Silver Dagger

Silver Dagger

David French

Talonbooks • **Vancouver** • **1993**

published with the assistance of the Canada Council

Talonbooks
201 / 1019 East Cordova Street
Vancouver, British Columbia
V6A 1M8 Canada

Typeset in Baskerville. Printed and bound in Canada by Hignell Printing Ltd.

First printing: May 1993

Canadian Cataloguing in Publication Data

French, David 1939-
    Silver dagger

    A play.
    ISBN 0-88922-325-4

    I. Title.
PS8561.R44S5 1993 C812'.54   C92-091208-X
PR9199.3.F73S5 1993

Silver Dagger was a co-production of The Canadian Stage
Company in Toronto and The National Arts Centre in
Ottawa. It opened at the Bluma Appel Theatre in Toronto on
January 4th, 1993, with the following cast:

JANE TALBOT	Brenda Robins
PAM MARSH	Kate Trotter
STEVE MARSH	Andrew Gillies
CHRIS DODD	Helen Taylor
TONY BISHOP	Randy Hughson
GEMMA DODD	Philippa Domville

Directed by Bill Glassco
Set and Costumes by John Ferguson
Lighting Designed by Kevin Fraser
Original Music Composed and Performed by Bill Thompson
Fight Director: John Stead
Assistant Director: Christopher McHarge

Silver Dagger transferred to the National Arts Centre in
Ottawa and opened there on February 4, 1993.

The Scene

The action takes place in the library of a house in
Toronto's Rosedale

Act One

Act Two

ACT ONE

SCENE ONE

Lights up on the large oak-paneled library of a house in mid-Toronto. The furniture consists of a sofa and wing chair, a floor lamp, a coffee table on which rests a silver dagger on a small stand, etcetera . . . A writing desk is at stage right. On the desk is a laptop computer. Against one wall is a buffet with liquor decanter, bottles, etcetera. Against another wall is a floor-to-ceiling bookcase.

Upstage right is a row of windows, hung with drapes, allowing us a view of the trees behind the house. French doors open onto a patio. Stage left is the fireplace. On the mantle is a small ceramic bust of Edgar Allan Poe. Upstage left is the entrance to the library, with sliding doors. We can glimpse the hall and the staircase that leads up to the second floor. The front door is unseen.

It is a few minutes after twelve o'clock noon, of a lovely day in May. The sun streams in the windows.

At rise, two women are on stage. PAM MARSH, the mistress of the house, is seated on the sofa, absorbed in reading her late father's will. PAM is in her mid-thirties, someone quite capable of navigating the maze of a legal document and carrying on a conversation at the same time. She is dressed simply but tastefully, with no hint of mourning in her dress or manner.

JANE TALBOT, PAM's lawyer, stands at the bookcase, scanning a shelf of hardcover mystery novels. Her coat is folded neatly over the back of the wing chair, on which rests her briefcase. JANE is roughly the same age as PAM, and since the two women are friends, there is a natural ease between them . . . JANE selects a book, removes it from the shelf, and studies the dustjacket.

JANE:

> *Cry Blue Murder.* Is this the one they made into a TV movie?

PAM:

> No. That was his last one, *Naked To The Hangman's Noose.* Poor Steven. He could barely watch it.

JANE:

> Oh?

PAM:

> The Inspector was all wrong. Far too glamorous. Remember how he's described in the book?

JANE:

> I have to confess I've never read either of his novels. Isn't that awful?

PAM:

> That's my fault. The best way to keep a friend from reading a book is to recommend it.

JANE:

> Don't be so cynical. . . .   *(She flicks open the book, glances at the first page, then begins to read)*   'The girl was no more than sixteen, if that. She lay on her back at the foot of the tree, with the cold March rain beating down on her, her eyes staring straight up at the rain, unblinking. There was a small red hole in her left temple, Sharpe noticed. The blood had washed away in the rain.' Not bad.   *(She returns the book to the shelf)*

PAM:
He's very gifted, Steven. The trouble is the literati don't
take him seriously. He's considered a genre writer. As if
the limitations of a form can't be transcended.

JANE:
P.D. James. John Le Carré.

PAM:
Exactly. My course in Detective Fiction is still frowned
on by the academic snobs. Universities aren't supposed
to take that kind of writing seriously . . .

JANE:
Will it cost you the promotion, do you think?

PAM:
I hope not. I know I have enemies there who don't like
the fact that I speak my mind. Some of them may envy
my wealth and privilege. Others just resent it . . .
(Finishing the will, she tosses it on the coffee table)
Finally.

JANE:
Any questions?

PAM:
I can't think of any. Not at the moment.

JANE:
You understand, Pam, that the will has to be probated.
All your father's assets — including this house — have
to be transferred from his estate to your name. It's
going to take some time, but in the end you'll be filthy
rich.

PAM:
>Want to know something, Jane? I don't know what I'll do with all that wealth. Just living here for the past few months has made me terribly uncomfortable. It's far too grand.

JANE:
>Oh, that's just the academic in you, embarrassed to be living in Rosedale. Does Steve feel the same way?

PAM:
>Steven? No, he loves it. He put his stuff in here and settled right in as if he belonged. Drink?

JANE:
>Make it Perrier. I have to be in court.

PAM: (*making the drinks*)
>One thing did surprise me, now that I think of it. About the will, I mean.

JANE:
>What's that?

PAM:
>Well, it's no secret Daddy didn't trust Steven. That's why he insisted I have a Pre-nuptial Agreement.

JANE:
>He saw every suitor as a gold-digger.

PAM:
>That's just my point. If my father was so concerned about Steven getting his hands on my inheritance, why isn't that in the will?

JANE:

There was no need. In effect, the Pre-nuptial excludes Steve from ever sharing your inheritance. Remember, it stipulates that if you and Steve ever divorce, Steve will get little more than what he brought to the marriage.

PAM:

Which is not a lot.

JANE:

Exactly. Unless, of course, you wanted to be generous. You could rescind the contract, remember.

PAM:

No, I don't think I'll do that. Not just yet, anyway. *(She hands JANE her Perrier)* But God, it would be nice if he had some money of his own. For his own sake . . . *(Off, we hear the front door open and close)* I think that's the Great Man now . . .

JANE: *(meaning the will)*

You can keep that copy. I have another in the safe.

STEVE MARSH enters, a youthful man in his early forties.

STEVE:

I don't suppose the garage called?

PAM:

Sorry, darling. Not yet.

STEVE:

Dammit. They promised I'd have the car back today. I'm lost without wheels . . . *(He crosses to the buffet, pours himself a Scotch, and belts it back)*

13

JANE:

So how did the interview go? Or dare I ask?

STEVE:

You mean you two didn't watch it?

PAM:

We were busy, so I taped it.

STEVE:

Burn the tape. The mortified author has crawled home, bleeding from all of his bodily orifices. Like a beaten cur.

JANE:

Oh, my.

STEVE pours another Scotch.

PAM:

Easy does it, Steven.

STEVE:

What was it Chekhov said? 'The stage is a scaffold on which the playwright hangs himself.' The same, dear friends, could be said for crime writers who appear on TV.

PAM:

It was that bad?

STEVE:

Worse. The red light went on, and the host said, 'Today's first guest is mystery writer, Steve Marsh. Steve's third novel has just been published and he's joined us today to discuss his work. 'Steve,' he said, 'let's begin by talking about your book. Could you tell us the title?' . . . And I looked at him, looked at his bland, decent face, at the little crescent scar below his right eye, and suddenly I heard this tiny voice that I didn't recognize, coming out from the end of a tunnel, 'Would you mind repeating the question, Ted?' (It turned out his name was Bill). And I saw the light in his eyes make a sudden shift, and I knew that shift was fear. It was as if I'd whipped out your father's .45 automatic and set it between us on the table. Suddenly there was this large drop of sweat on the tip of his nose, and this large drop of sweat on the tip of mine. 'The title of your novel, Steve? Could you tell our audience the title, please?' I said, 'I know you'll think this is silly, Fred, but I forget . . .' And the poor fellow began to hyperventilate. They had to go to commercial . . .

JANE:
Oh, God, I would just die, if that were me. No wonder you need a double Scotch.

PAM:
Don't be so gullible, Jane. Can't you see he made it up?

JANE:
Made what up?

PAM:
Oh, he did the interview all right. But it didn't happen as Steven so gleefully described it. Did it, darling?

STEVE:
I may put that into a book, though. Now that I know it works.

PAM:
He does that a lot. Tries stuff out on me.

STEVE:
Apparently they liked me. I came across as a man of modest ambition, a sort of wetback in the field of literature. At first the host was somewhat patronizing. Then when he convinced himself he was more intelligent, he relaxed and was generous. Once or twice he mentioned my *oeuvre* — his word, not mine — and to be fair, he said it without wrinkling his nose or making it sound like something lodged in my large intestine.

JANE: *(to PAM)*
Tell me: how did you know Steve was lying?

STEVE:
I prefer fabricating, if you don't mind. As in fiction . . .
(To PAM) Yes, Inspector Sharpe, where *did* I go wrong?

PAM:
Natural Causes, my darling.

JANE:
Natural causes?

PAM: *(shows her a copy of the book)*
The title of the latest Inspector Sharpe of the Metropolitan Toronto Police.

JANE:
I don't understand.

STEVE:
I think I do. Very clever, Pamela. And readers wonder who the inspector is modeled on?

JANE:
I still don't get it.

PAM:

It's simple. This was a major TV spot, and yet Steven
said the host kept asking for the title of his new book.
That's the detail that didn't ring true.

JANE:

Why not?

PAM:

Because his publisher would've made damn sure the
host had a copy to hold up for the camera. Right,
Steven?

STEVE:

This is Canada, don't forget: *I* provided the book. Most
publishers think it's enough to publish the damn thing.
They believe they're being bullied if you expect them to
sell it.

JANE:

Well, you had me fooled, I must say. I think you should
make acting a second career.

PAM:

He almost did.

STEVE:

I played Petruchio in a student production of *The
Taming of the Shrew.* I even fooled the critics.

The phone rings. STEVE answers it.

STEVE:

Hello . . . Yes, it is. . . . Oh, you did? Well, thank you. I
thought I came off rather poorly . . . Sorry, I didn't
catch your name . . . Which magazine? . . . Ah, *Quill &
Quire* . . . Oh, God, I detest phone interviews. And my
car's being fixed or I'd suggest we meet somewhere.

Just a minute . . . *(Covers the handset)* It's a
woman from *Quill & Quire*. They're doing a piece on
me in the next issue. She's desperate to interview me.

PAM:
Tell her to come here.

STEVE:
Thanks, darling . . . *(Into the phone)* Look,
Chris, is it? Why don't you come here? I hate talking to
a voice I can't put a face to . . . Yes, it's 78 Oak Park
Road. Overlooking the ravine. You can't miss it. It's at
the end of a cul-de-sac . . . Where are you now? . . . Oh,
good. That shouldn't take too long . . . Right. See you
anon. *(He hangs up)*

PAM:
See you anon?

STEVE:
I know. I'm beginning to talk like Sergeant Nash. Either
I break myself of the habit or kill him off, the pompous
twit . . . *(He exits upstairs)*

JANE:
My God, but his mind works fast. He must've made up
that story as soon as he realized we hadn't watched the
show.

PAM:
With Steven, it's hard to know what to believe. He likes
to keep you off balance.

JANE:
I'd love to have him for a witness. Most of my clients
have no imagination, especially for detail . . .
(Glances at her watch) Speaking of work, I've got a

case in court at two. I still have to review my client's testimony. *(She slips on her coat)*

PAM:

Must you rush off? I was hoping we'd get a chance to talk.

JANE:

We'll have lunch soon. I promise. I want to hear every last bit of juicy gossip. *(She picks up her briefcase, locks it, and pecks PAM on the cheek)* Oh, and say goodbye to Steve for me, I . . . *(PAM turns abruptly away)* What is it? What's wrong? *(Then)* Pam?

PAM: *(beat)*

Actually, it was Steven I wanted to talk about. *(Beat)* I think he's seeing another woman.

JANE:

Oh, dear.

PAM:

Is that all you can say?

JANE:

Pam, you caught me off guard.

PAM:

He denies it, of course. Too vehemently, I might add. Says I'm paranoid.

JANE:

You've confronted him?

PAM:

Naturally I've confronted him. But you saw what an accomplished liar he is.

JANE:
Then what makes you suspect he's having an affair?

PAM:
Oh, nothing as cliché as a name on a matchbox. Or
lipstick stains . . .   *(She gives JANE her drink and crosses
to the desk . . . removes an envelope from the drawer)*   No,
this came in the mail last week. Addressed to me. I
don't recognize the handwriting.   *(She hands the
envelope to JANE, who removes the letter and reads it)*
And there have been phone calls lately. I pick up the
phone, and no one's there.

JANE: *(reads aloud)*
'No man worth having is true to his wife, or can be true
to his wife, or ever was, or ever will be.' A quote?

PAM:
I looked it up. Sir John Vanbrugh. Seventeenth Century
English playwright.

JANE:
Sounds like Sir John's one helluva cynic for a knight . . .
Oh, look, Pam, I wouldn't get all worked up. This
could've been sent by anyone. An old disgruntled lover.
His or yours. Even a sick fan.

PAM:
You think so?

JANE:
Are you kidding? Celebrities get worse things in the
mail than quotations. I know a model who sends her ex-
husband used condoms with little name-tags on them.

PAM:
What about the phone calls?

JANE:

All women get calls like that. One old judge has been phoning me for ages, I recognize his breathing.

PAM:

So you think I'm overreacting?

JANE:

Let's put it this way. If a Crown Attorney went to trial with evidence this flimsy, they'd toss out the case . . . Frankly, I don't believe a word of it. So there . . . Anyway, I have to go. We'll talk again soon.

PAM:

Thanks, Jane. I mean it.

JANE:

Just out of curiosity, what would happen if you found it were true? That Steve was fooling around?

PAM:

I think you already know the answer, don't you?

JANE:

You're forgetting one thing, Pam. You and Steve have that Marriage Contract. You think he's going to risk all this for a piece of crumpet?

PAM:

Men have done it before.

JANE:

Not Steve. You just love him too much, Pammy. That's why you're imagining all this. 'Bye for now.   (She exits, only to reappear a few seconds later, holding a small batch of mail)   Your mail's here. I thought you'd want

to look through it . . .   *(Hands it to PAM)*   I
promise: No more false exits.   *(And she's gone)*

> *PAM looks through the mail. There are no more anony-*
> *mous letters, and she seems relieved. She tosses the mail on*
> *an endtable. Just then, the phone rings. It startles her. It*
> *rings again. PAM walks over, hesitates, and after the third*
> *ring, picks up the handset.*

PAM:
Hello . . . Oh, yes . . . Oh, good . . . Yes, we'll be here . . .
Alright, I'll tell him. Goodbye.   *(She hangs up)*

> *During this, STEVE comes down the stairs. He is now*
> *wearing a tweed jacket with leather elbow patches and has*
> *changed his shirt and put on a tie.*

PAM:
That was the garage. They're sending over the car. I
think that's pretty decent of them, don't you?

STEVE:
One of the boys fancies himself a writer. He likes to talk
shop . . . This all the mail?

PAM:
Most if it's bills. A few things are for you.

> *STEVE scoops up the mail and drops onto the sofa. He*
> *begins to attack the letters with a steel letter-opener.*

STEVE:
Here's one from a German publisher enquiring about
Cry Blue Murder. Someone wants to translate it . . . Ah,
another review of *Natural Causes.* Oh, good.   *(Reads)*
'NATURAL CAUSES DAZZLES.' The title could have worked
against me, of course. 'MARSH'S REPUTATION DIES OF

NATURAL CAUSES.' I'll have to watch that in future . . .
(He continues to read his mail)

Slight pause.

PAM:
Steven.

STEVE:
Mmm.

PAM:
Someone called again this morning. Right after you
left . . . *(STEVE flashes her an impatient look)* I
just thought you should know . . . It's so unnerving.
Knowing someone's on the other end. Just listening.

STEVE:
Why don't we get an unlisted number? That would put
a stop to it.

PAM:
It's also occurred to me that there may not be a
connection between the letter and the phone calls.
We just assumed there was.

STEVE:
You assumed that, not me.

PAM:
Jane thinks the phone calls are just part of modern life:
random.

STEVE:
Oh? Did you also discuss the letter with her?

PAM:
Why wouldn't I discuss it? Jane's a friend of mine.

STEVE:
Who else have you told, Pamela? *People Magazine?* The *National Enquirer?*

PAM:
Why are you getting upset?

STEVE:
I'll tell you why. Because I don't like the cavalier way you expose our private lives. And I don't care if she is a friend. Besides, I thought she was here on business, not to play Dear Abby.

PAM:
Jane happens to be on your side, in case you're interested. And she said more or less the same thing you did. That it's probably the work of a crazy person.

STEVE:
And Jane you believe.

PAM:
Come on, Steven, that's not fair. It's not that I don't trust you, it's just . . .

STEVE:
What?

PAM:
I don't face the same temptations you do. I'm not interviewed on TV. I don't get fan mail from tasty little morsels.

STEVE:

So what? You're a beautiful woman. Is it so far-fetched to imagine one of your colleagues might not be the guilty party? Knowing he'd stand a better chance with you if your husband weren't in the picture?

PAM:

Sorry. That only happens in books.

STEVE:

Alright, I'll give you an even better motive. How's this? Someone in your department knows you're being considered for full professor. He wants to sabotage your promotion any way he can. Maybe fan the flames of scandal. And don't tell me it's far-fetched, Pam. You're an academic, you know how vicious those people can be . . . *(He takes an envelope from the inside pocket of his jacket and hands it to her)* I was trying to find the right time to give you this, but it's never the right time, I suppose. Another quote from your Pen Pal.

PAM:

Where did you get it?

STEVE:

Read it.

PAM:

This has been opened . . .

STEVE:

Look, just read it, and then you can scream at me . . . When I came home, the mail was in the hall. So I took the letter. I wanted to read it before you did . . .

PAM: *(reads aloud)*

'His designs were strictly honourable, as the phrase is: that is, to rob a lady of her fortune by way of marriage.'

25

STEVE:
You recognize it?

PAM:
Sounds like Fielding. Probably *Tom Jones.*

STEVE:
Both quotes are from dead authors. I'm telling you, Pam, it's got to be someone in the English Department. Some jealous colleague. Or maybe a moonstruck grad. student.

PAM:
Why didn't you destroy this?

STEVE:
I was going to, but then I realized the only antidote to this kind of poison is honesty. He can't hurt us unless we allow him to . . . Anyway, I know it was wrong of me to read your mail. For that, I apologize.

PAM:
Oh, honey, I wish I weren't so hard on you. No, Steven, I'm the one who should apologize. I just get so damnably insecure at times. Forgive me?

STEVE:
Let's forget it, shall we? I might be jealous, too, under the circumstances. But the fact is we're very happy together. Why would I want to have an affair?
(He kisses her)

PAM:
Look, I have a wonderful idea. I have that conference in two weeks. Why don't you come with me? It's been so long since we had any time together. Especially in the Caribbean.

STEVE:
You know I can't, sweetheart. As much as I'd like to. I've promised to do that promotion tour. I can't suddenly back out now.

Doorbell.

PAM:
Finish your mail. I'll get that.   *(She exits into the hall)*

STEVE: *(picks up a letter and reads aloud)*
. . . 'My roommate wanted to invite you over, but she said you probably wouldn't like to come, since we're two single girls and you're married. Was she right?' Wrong. *(He crumples the letter)*

> *At that moment, PAM ushers in CHRIS DODD, an attractive young woman in her mid-twenties, with short blond hair and wire-rimmed glasses. CHRIS carries a tape recorder on a shoulder strap, and appears shy and awkward, as though slightly out of her depth. STEVE puts aside his mail and rises with a smile to greet her.*

PAM:
Steven, this is Chris . . .   *(Turns to CHRIS for help)*

CHRIS: *(to STEVE)*
Dodd. Hi . . .   *(Shakes hands)*   Sorry about this, I know it's last minute, I won't take much of your . . .

PAM:
Relax, dear. The truth is he enjoys the attention.

CHRIS: *(to PAM)*
To be honest, this is only my second assignment . . .

STEVE:

I see you brought along a tape recorder. Good thinking.

CHRIS:

I don't trust my memory, and my shorthand's not that great. Well, you know. Then again, you wouldn't, would you? You probably have a photographic memory.

PAM:

Only for reviews, my dear. The bad ones.

STEVE:

The good ones I never remember.

PAM:

I'll leave you two alone. I'll be in my office, darling. *(As she goes)* Don't let my husband intimidate you, Miss Dodd, his bark is worse than his bite.

She exits upstairs.

CHRIS:

Is that true, Mr. Marsh? Is your bark worse than your bite?

STEVE:

It was you who wrote those letters, wasn't it? . . . Well? . . . Christ, you really like to push your luck, don't you? What if my wife had recognized you?

CHRIS:

Recognized me? How?

STEVE:

Idiot. She saw *Hangman's Noose.* You're not exactly the type that fades into the background.

CHRIS:
Get real. I had a small part.

STEVE:
There are no small parts. Just roles that can land me in Divorce Court. God, how can you be so bloody stupid! *(Pours himself a Scotch)*

CHRIS:
She can't hear us, can she?

STEVE:
Of course not. No, her office is on the third floor. You think I'd be talking like this if she could?

CHRIS:
By the way, Steve, I really admire the way you improvise. An interview with *Quill & Quire!*

STEVE:
I had to think of something, didn't I? You said you were on your way over. And either I talked to you or you talked to Pam. That tends to prime my creative pump.

CHRIS:
I thought it best we talk here . . . I've never had the part of a journalist before. You don't think I overdid the gauche young thing, do you?

STEVE:
I gather you're the one who's been calling here?

CHRIS:
Always from a phone booth.

STEVE:
What were the letters meant to do, tighten the screws? Soften me up for blackmail?

CHRIS:
Is that what you think this is?

STEVE:
Isn't it?

CHRIS:
I prefer to call it compensation. Payment for the way you treated my sister. Tell me, Steve. When did you first know it was me? When I called just now?

STEVE:
Yes. Until then I was convinced it was someone from the university. Gemma's not the type to resort to blackmail.

CHRIS:
Of course not. And just in case you're thinking of telling her, I'd think twice. You tell Gemma, I tell Pam. Fair enough?

STEVE:
Listen, I never meant to hurt your sister, no matter what you think. The truth is we cared for each other a great deal. More than you know.

CHRIS:
That's why you dumped her? Because you cared for her? Who do you think you're conning, Steve, your biographer? You can fool your wife, your shrink, even yourself, but don't include me. Did you know she tried to kill herself that night?

STEVE:
Gemma? . . .

CHRIS:
I found her in the bathtub. She'd cut her wrists. She was just sitting there, in the dark.

STEVE:

    Christ.

CHRIS:

    Some day I'll describe that night in detail. Being a
    writer, you might find it interesting . . . Maybe you can
    put it in one of your books.

STEVE:

    I don't understand. Gemma and I had always been
    honest with each other. It's not as though she thought
    we had a future together.

CHRIS:

    Get off it, Steve. She was no different than any other
    woman in love. She believed you'd give up your wife . . .
    (STEVE says nothing)   Maybe I'm somewhat to blame.
    After all, I introduced you.

STEVE:

    Look, just what is it you want, Chris? And you can drop
    the sisterly act, okay? Gemma told me how you feel
    about her.

CHRIS:

    It's like that, is it? In that case, let's get down to business.
    What I want, Steve, is fifty thousand dollars. Cash.

STEVE:

    You're out of your mind.

CHRIS:

    Fifty thousand almost makes up for what I went through
    with Gemma. I don't like being miscast in the role of
    ministering angel. Besides, I have an agent now in L.A.
    I plan to move there and look for work. Fifty thousand
    should tide me over quite nicely.

STEVE:
Where the hell would I get that kind of money? I'm a writer, not a dentist. In fact, if I wasn't married to Pam, I'd still be teaching high school and writing novels that no one would publish.

CHRIS:
An amount like that shouldn't be hard to raise. Not for someone who lives like this . . . *(She indicates the room)*

STEVE:
This is my wife's house, not mine. At least it will be hers, when her father's will is probated.

CHRIS:
She'll inherit all he has, won't she? I read there are no other living relatives.

STEVE:
Just what do you expect me to do? Go to my wife and say, 'Sorry dear, the sister of a woman I had an affair with is blackmailing me. Can you loan me fifty grand to pay her off?'

CHRIS:
How much do you have?

STEVE:
I don't know. I might be able to scrape together fifteen, but I'd need time.

CHRIS:
How much time?

STEVE:
A few weeks.

CHRIS:

    Alright. But remember, fifteen's just the down
payment. Oh, and Steve, I know how cunning you can
be. I can imagine you confessing the whole thing to
Pam . . . casting yourself as the innocent victim of blackmail. After all, there's no real evidence against you, is
there?

STEVE:

    True. It's really your word against mine. And Gemma
would deny the affair ever happened.

CHRIS:

    However, you just made one mistake, Steve, and it's a
costly one. You see, this tape recorder's not just a prop.
I've recorded everything we've said since your wife left
the room. If you try anything funny, I'll make sure Pam
gets the tape. Understand?

STEVE: *(beat)*

    I've underestimated you, haven't I?

CHRIS:

    Arrogant people tend to do that . . . So just make sure
you get the money, Steve, or you'll be back teaching
Great Expectations to kids who'd sooner watch the video.

    Doorbell.

STEVE:

    Are we finished? Because I have other business to
attend to.

CHRIS:

    I'll be in touch.

STEVE:
Take your time. And on your way out, send in Tony,
would you? He's an ex-con. Don't get too close, I don't
want him corrupted.

*CHRIS exits. STEVE sits at the desk and gets out his
chequebook. TONY BISHOP enters, carrying in one hand
a clipboard on which is attached a large manila envelope
and an invoice. In the other hand he holds a hardcover
book in its dustjacket. TONY is 28 years old, athletic
looking. He wears a blue denim shirt, dark slacks, loafers
and a wide grin. His glance soaks up the room.*

TONY:
Whoa. This is some place, Mr. Marsh. Writing books
must be lucrative. Not like working in Harry's
Autobody.

STEVE:
Cut the crap, Tony. Just give me the bad news, I'm
sitting down.

TONY:
Here's the invoice: it's itemized . . .   *(Hands it to
STEVE)*   New rear tire. Front wheel alignment.
Must've hit a pothole . . . And brake fluid. With tax,
$546.18.

STEVE:
Harry's a thief.

TONY:
I know. He's a New Age Robin Hood. He steals from the
rich and keeps it . . .   *(As STEVE writes the cheque,
TONY wanders about the room)*   If you don't mind me
asking, Mr. Marsh, who was that woman who was just
here? She looked familiar.

STEVE:
How do you know she's not my wife?

TONY: *(indicating a framed picture on the endtable)*
Well, I figure Mrs. Marsh is this lady here in the picture.
I say that because she's in the wedding dress and you're
in the tux.

STEVE:
Very observant . . . No, the young woman's a journalist.
Writes for the magazine, *Quill & Quire.*

TONY:
Funny. I could've sworn I'd seen her before. I don't
forget a face. Maybe she looks like someone else. We're
all supposed to have a twin somewhere, aren't we?
Imagine that, Mr. Marsh. Some guy's walking around
right now, my lookalike, only he's driving a Porsche, the
sonofabitch, a Rolex watch on his left wrist. If I ever
meet him, I'll kill him and takes his place . . .   *(By
now he is at the fireplace. He removes the bust of Edgar Allan
Poe from the mantle and caresses it)*   Oh, wow, this is the
Edgar Allan Poe Award they gave you for *Cry Blue
Murder.* Very nice.

STEVE:
Be careful: it's ceramic.   *(He crosses to TONY and
hands him the cheque. He takes the Edgar from TONY and
puts it back on the mantle)*   I don't think the Mystery
Writers of America would replace that, if I broke it.

TONY:
Listen, I have a confession to make. When Harry asked
me to drop off your car, I rushed home and got *Natural
Causes.* I wonder if you'd mind autographing it.

STEVE:
My pleasure. *(He takes the book, sits on the sofa, and begins to scribble on the title page)*

TONY:
You know, not many writers win a Silver Dagger. *(He takes the Silver Dagger from the coffee table and holds it reverently)* Especially not for a second novel.

STEVE:
Pure luck.

TONY:
Luck, my foot. You're a gifted man of letters, Mr. Marsh. Who just happens to use the mystery genre to explore the Great Themes of Western Man. In other words, you're a serious novelist of the first rank and deserve to be treated as such.

STEVE:
Call me Steve.

TONY:
For what it's worth, Steve, I have a hunch you'll cop the Gold Dagger for *Natural Causes*. Even my mother couldn't put it down, and she hardly ever reads. *(He sets the Silver Dagger back on the coffee table)*

STEVE: *(hands back the book)*
She liked it, did she?

TONY:
What's not to like? For one thing, it's fast-paced and superbly crafted. For another, it's full of suspense, surprises, and pithy insights. I can't remember a book that made my hands sweat and my heart pound. It was like sex.

STEVE:

Maybe you should write the copy for my next dust-jacket.

TONY: *(reads aloud the inscription)*

'For Tony Bishop, may he one day make it into print. Best wishes, Steve Marsh' . . . It's funny you should say that, Steve, I just finished the first chapter of a crime novel. And I was wondering if maybe you could read it . . . *(Indicates the manila envelope)*

STEVE:

I might've known. Flattery always comes with a price tag, doesn't it? Well, the answer is no, Tony. I make it a rule never to read work from new writers. Never.

TONY:

All I want is criticism, Steve.

STEVE:

Criticism? Writer's don't want criticism, they want praise. If I tell you it's less than perfect, you'll go home in a snit. From that day forward you'll regard me as a hack.

TONY:

Hey, I'm not like that. To bat in the Major Leagues, first you got to know how to stand . . . how to swing. And maybe I don't belong in the dugout. Maybe I'll always be a Bat Boy.

STEVE:

Spare me the baseball metaphor, it's been done to death.

TONY:

I need to know if I have any talent. Besides, you're the only writer I know, Steve. You're the one that made me want to write crime fiction.

STEVE:

Don't hustle me, Tony.

TONY:

It's true. Someone in the joint had one of your books, *Cry Blue Murder*. That novel changed my life. Hey, I don't want to sound like a Baptist, but man, I had a real conversion. Like Saul on the road to Damascus.

STEVE:

Cry Blue Murder did that?

TONY:

Yes, sir, it did. I remember the night I read that book. I had the closest thing to an epiphany I've ever felt or ever expect to feel.

STEVE:

An epiphany? Oh, my.

TONY:

I know. You probably think I'm full of it. Spiritual talk embarrasses me, too.

STEVE:

You expect me to believe you had a revelation? Reading a book about murder and mayhem?   *(He pours two glasses of Scotch)*

TONY:

I know it sounds crazy, but that's what happened. From the moment I read *Cry Blue Murder* I knew what I wanted to be: a writer. The fact I was a car thief and burglar never even occurred to me. No, it was as if I'd stepped out of my skin, suddenly, and left my old self behind me on the road. Like a snake. It was as if I'd walked through a door and into a world that had always been there, always, only I just didn't know it. God, it looked so clean to me, suddenly. The world, I mean. Clean and bright the way it gets sometime when you've had too much to drink. Or you've taken mescaline. Like that.

STEVE:
I just want to ask one thing, Tony. Are you bullshitting me?

TONY:
The Gospel truth, Steve. I swear. From that night on I wanted to be a writer more than I'd ever wanted anything in my life. I wanted to write mysteries, the kind that kept the reader up half the night, just the way you did with me. You see, Steve, you may not know it, my friend, but that night in Joyceville you gave me something I can't ever repay. You gave me back my life . . .   *(Snaps his fingers)*   That's it! That's who she is!

STEVE:
Who?

TONY:
That girl who was just here. She's not a reporter, she's an actress. She played the schoolteacher in *Naked To The Hangman's Noose.*

STEVE:
That's impossible.

TONY:
I'm telling you, Steve. I remember her.

STEVE:
And I'm telling you she's not the same person. Why the hell would I lie about a thing like that? Why?

TONY:
I don't know. All I know is the actress who played the Amish teacher is the same person I just met at the front door. And it's not only her face I recognize, it's the voice. Believe me, I never forget a voice . . .   *(STEVE says nothing)*   I'm right, aren't I, Steve?   *(Then)* Aren't I?

STEVE: *(hands TONY the Scotch)*
Sit down, and I'll explain . . .   *(TONY sits)*   The fact is, Tony, I need a favour. Only it's not the sort of favour your Parole Officer would approve. Understand?

TONY:
She's blackmailing you, right?

STEVE:
You're not only observant, you're intuitive. Yes, she's blackmailing me. And if my wife were ever to find out . . . Well, I've grown quite fond of this house. I'd hate to have to give it up.

Blackout.

SCENE TWO

*A week later. Night. It is storming outside. The only light
on stage spills in from the hall. Suddenly the stage is lit in
a brilliant burst of lightning, and we can see the drapes
have not been drawn. Rain streaks down the glass. A
moment later, we hear PAM and STEVE rush in the front
door, laughing. We hear them hang up their coats, etcetera . . .
Finally, STEVE enters the library and flicks on the light.
Thunder rumbles.*

STEVE:
What a night. Right out of Bram Stoker.

PAM: *(entering)*
I know. Don't you just love it?   *(She goes around
clicking on the table lamps)*

STEVE pours himself a Scotch.

STEVE:
Scotch?

PAM:
Make it a brandy.

STEVE:
Christ, what an abysmal production. The set was the
pits, the cast was all wrong, the costumes were drab, the
lighting designer, I swear, has cataracts —

PAM:
The blocking wasn't bad.

STEVE:
Oh, come on. All those group pictures that had nothing
to do with anything but the director's sense of stage
composition. I can't remember a single move that was

psychologically motivated. And whoever was in the booth ought to be shot. I counted three missed light cues and two missed sound cues. All in all, I had a perfectly delightful time, didn't you?   (*Hands her the brandy*)

PAM:

No, I didn't. Not being a friend of the author I don't take the same pleasure in watching his play go down the drain.

STEVE:

Just watch. It'll get raves! . . .   (*At the answering machine*)   Three messages. Aren't we popular. (*He presses the play button*)

JANE'S VOICE:

Hi, Pam, it's Jane. Let me know if Tuesday's okay for lunch. Call me at the office tomorrow, I'm out for the night. Thanks. Bye . . .

TONY'S VOICE:

Steve, this is Tony Bishop. It's eight-thirty. I'll call you later . . .

PAM:

Who is that, Steven? I think he's the one who called here this morning.

TONY'S VOICE:

Steve, it's me again, Tony. It's ten o'clock. I really need to see you tonight. I'll keep trying . . .

PAM:

He wouldn't leave his name or number.

STEVE:
Remember the mechanic who dropped off the car last week? That's Tony Bishop. Grease monkey and ex-con. The one who's been bitten by the literary bug.

PAM:
Pity there's no vaccine . . . What does he want?

STEVE:
From me? Validation. I agreed to read the first chapter of a book he's writing. Now I'm supposed to tell him it's the best thing since *The Moonstone*.

PAM:
How is it really?

STEVE:
Well, if I tell him the truth, he'll hate me. If I lie to him, I'll hate myself. The usual dilemma.

PAM:
Do what I do, darling: Say it's interesting.

STEVE:
That's fine for academics, Pam. Writers are supposed to have scruples. No, I wonder why he's calling tonight of all nights? He's not usually that persistent . . .   *(He bites his thumbnail, stops when he catches PAM watching)*

PAM: *(crossing to fix herself another brandy)*
I've noticed you doing that a lot lately. In all the time I've known you, Steven, you've never once bitten your nails.

STEVE:
Listen, love, I've begun a new book. You know what a terrifying time that is for me . . .

PAM:
> Still, it's not like you to talk in your sleep. I've never
> known you to do that, either.

STEVE:
> I talked in my sleep? When?

PAM:
> Last night. Well, not talked, exactly. You cried out.

STEVE:
> Oh? What did I say?

PAM:
> You didn't say anything. Why do you ask?

STEVE:
> Oh, come on, Pam. I thought we'd resolved all that.
> The phone calls have stopped, and the letters. Now you
> make it sound as though you suspect me of something.

PAM:
> Steven, I'm not the sort of wife who goes through your
> pockets, but don't expect me not to pick up on verbal
> nuances. The fact is you asked that question just now as
> if you might've said something you shouldn't . . .

STEVE:
> Oh, for God's sake! . . .

PAM:
> Don't you patronize me, dammit!

STEVE:
> Alright, I confess. Your friend Jane and I have been
> meeting secretly for years. We plan to do away with you,

44

maybe tonight, and bury your body in the ravine.
Satisfied?

There is a roll of thunder.

PAM:
At one time I might have believed you. I used to think
that you and Jane were getting it on. But she's not really
your type, is she?

STEVE:
You actually thought Talbot and I were lovers? Why the
hell would you think that?

PAM:
Are you aware that you hardly ever look at each other?
That's often a dead give away that something is going
on.

STEVE:
I don't believe it. Who else have you got on my list of
paramours? The girl from *Quill & Quire?*

PAM:
Alright, I'm insecure. I admit it.

STEVE:
No kidding. Christ, remember what you did to that PR
girl at my book launching? You publicly humiliated her,
and without cause.

PAM:
I still think I was right.

STEVE:
Oh, come on. You hurled your Mouton Cadet in her
face, all because she picked some lint off my suit.

PAM:
Don't be naive, Steven. A woman who picks thread off a
man's lapel is not studying to be a tailor. Nor is she
probably any more obsessive than most. She's just being
intimate in a way that's provocative. Besides, it wasn't
just that. It was the way she was rubbing herself against
you. Like she was a bear and you were a tree.

A tremendous flash of lightning makes even PAM wince.

PAM:
The storm's getting worse . . .   *(She starts towards the
windows to draw the drapes, when another flash reveals a
figure peering in through the rain-streaked glass. PAM cries
out and points)*

STEVE: *(sets down his drink)*
What? What is it?

PAM:
There's someone at the window!

STEVE: *(at the window)*
Are you sure?

PAM:
Of course I'm sure. He was peering in.

*STEVE crosses to the desk and gets a small handgun from
the drawer.*

PAM:
What are you doing?

STEVE:
Turn off the light.

STEVE crosses to the windows. PAM flicks off the main light, leaving only the table lamps to illumine the room. STEVE presses his face to the glass and peers out.

PAM:
Do you see anything?

STEVE:
No. Nothing.

PAM:
He was there. I saw him.

> *STEVE unhooks the French doors. Takes an umbrella from the stand.*

PAM:
You can't go out there, Steven. Let's just call the police.

STEVE:
Let me check the garden first . . . Look, stop worrying, I'll be right back. Besides, it's probably nothing . . .
(Gun in hand, he disappears out into the night, leaving the door ajar)

> *The wind and rain blow in the room. Almost moaning with fright, PAM looks quickly around for a weapon. She picks up a poker. Another flash of lightning makes her jump. PAM moves slowly to the French doors. Another flash of lightning.*

PAM: *(calls out)*
Steven! Where are you? Steven!

Frightened, she crosses to the desk, picks up the phone, and begins to call the police. Suddenly a black umbrella rushes out of the night and PAM screams, slamming down the handset.

STEVE: *(entering)*
It's only me . . . Sorry if I frightened you.   *(He shakes the umbrella and returns it to the stand)*

PAM:
Thank God you're back. I was beginning to get worried.

STEVE:
Sorry, love. I checked the grounds. As far down as the gazebo.

PAM:
You didn't see anyone?

STEVE:
Not a soul. Look, are you sure it wasn't a branch you saw, or a shadow?

PAM:
It was not a shadow I saw, Steven. Or a branch. It was a man, and he had his face pressed to the window. For God's sake, close the door and put away that gun. It's making me nervous . . .

STEVE sets down the gun. He closes the French doors and draws the drapes. PAM flicks on the light.

STEVE:
Well, if someone was out there, he's gone now. Probably just some Peeping Tom.

Doorbell.

PAM:

Maybe the Peeping Tom's had enough for one night.
Maybe he wants a hot toddy and a change of socks.

STEVE:

Did you lock the front door?

PAM:

I always lock it. You know that . . .   *(STEVE picks up*
the gun and starts for the hall)   Be careful, Steven.

The doorbell sounds again. STEVE exits into the hall.
PAM crosses to the fireplace, still clutching the poker.

STEVE: *(off)*
Who is it?

A muffled shout from outside.

PAM:
Who?

STEVE: *(off)*
It's Tony Bishop.

PAM:
The mechanic?

STEVE: *(off)*
No, the writer. The mechanic's too bright to be out on a
night like this . . .   *(Thunder sounds and lightning*
cracks. A moment later, we catch a glimpse of STEVE and
TONY in the hall, STEVE helping TONY off with his

raincoat. Then he ushers TONY into the library)   Pam,
this is Tony Bishop. Tony, my wife, Pamela.

TONY:
My pleasure, Mrs. Marsh. Look, I'm sorry if I startled
you just now. I can explain what happened.

PAM:
Then it was you at the window, was it?

TONY:
Yes, Ma'am, it was. And I'm sorry if I frightened you.
Honestly.

STEVE:
You don't have to apologize, Tony. Besides, he didn't
frighten us, did he, darling?

PAM:
No, Steven always answers the door with a gun in his
hand. The rich can't be too careful, can they?

*STEVE takes the poker from PAM, then returns the gun to
the desk.*

TONY:
I wasn't sure if you were home or not. Your car wasn't in
the driveway, Steve, and the garage was locked. I didn't
want to ring the bell in case you were in bed. So I came
around to the library. You know, to see if you were still
up.

STEVE:
Where were you? I went all around the house. I didn't
see you.

TONY:
Oh, that. I guess I was covering my bike. It's parked across the street. I didn't want to put the tarp on till I knew for sure you were home.

PAM:
You're fortunate my husband didn't mistake you for a prowler.

STEVE:
Pam, why don't you make Tony a drink while I fetch his story? It's up in the bedroom.

PAM:
Yes, I'm sure he's dying to hear what you have to say. I know I am.

STEVE: *(as he goes)*
Frankly, I don't have much in the way of criticism. It's a damn good first effort. In fact, very interesting . . .
(He exits)

PAM:
One thing about Steven, he can always be counted on for an honest opinion. What would you like, Tony? Rum? Whiskey?

TONY:
Rye, if you have it. Straight.

PAM pours the drink.

TONY:
Steve tells me you're working on a book, Mrs. Marsh. Is that right? *From Wilkie Collins To Ruth Rendell: The Hero In Detective Fiction.*

PAM:

My, you certainly have a good memory, don't you? *(Hands him his drink)*   Not many would remember that.

TONY:

It's not that I have a good memory, Mrs. Marsh. It's just that I don't forget a catchy title. Especially one with a rolling cadence. Cheers.

PAM:

So you like the title, do you?

TONY:

It's brilliant. I wish I could come up with titles like that. I keep looking for mine in the King James Bible. But how many titles for thrillers can you find in *Ecclesiastes?*

Lightning strikes close by. PAM flinches.

PAM:

That must've hit the next street.

TONY:

Tonight reminds me of the thunderstorm in *The Spiral Staircase.* Ever see that film? The original, not the remake?

PAM:

I can't say I've had the pleasure.

TONY:

My mother keeps renting it. I don't know why she does that, it scares her silly.

PAM:

That's probably why she does it, it scares her silly.

TONY:

It takes place in New England at the turn of the
century. A serial killer is loose. He keeps strangling
young women. Girls with physical defects. Only we
don't know who the killer is, except when he's about to
strike, we hear this eerie music and the camera moves
in for a closeup of his eye. Just one crazed eye watching
his victim from the shadows.

PAM:

This is what your mother considers family entertain-
ment?

TONY:

Oh, it's great. The film's set in this dark old mansion,
and Dorothy McGuire plays the servant girl. The mute
servant girl, of course. Near the end she has to go down
to the cellar. So she lights a candle and down she goes,
down the spiral staircase to the cellar, this beautiful
young servant girl who can't cry out. And you want to
scream, 'No! Don't go down there alone! Don't go
down to the cellar!'

PAM:

On second thought, I might just skip that one.

TONY:

I won't tell you what happens next, except Dorothy
stumbles on another corpse. She's kneeling beside the
body when someone opens the cellar door. Wind
rushes in. Footsteps approach, and just when you think
you can't stand it a second longer . . .

PAM:

I know. Her candle goes out.

TONY:
Not quite. That happens later. No, she glances over her
shoulder, Dorothy does, and notices a pair of feet
planted firmly behind her . . .

PAM:
Look, Tony, I don't want to seem rude, but why did you
come here on a night like tonight? Something about
this just doesn't add up . . .

*Thunder. Lightning. STEVE enters, carrying TONY's
story in the manila envelope.*

STEVE:
Sorry about that. I scribbled down some notes, but I
can't seem to find them. Anyway, it doesn't matter . . .
(He hands TONY the envelope and picks up his drink)
As I mentioned before, it's a pretty interesting piece of
work. Flawed, but promising . . .

TONY:
Flawed?

STEVE:
Let me put it this way, Tony. The writer and the reader
have a covenant, and that covenant can't be broken,
ever. From the moment the reader begins the first
sentence, he agrees to a willing suspension of disbelief.
The writer, for his part, agrees never to abuse that trust.
Right, Pam?

TONY says nothing.

PAM:
Things must appear plausible. Isn't that what you're
trying to say, Steven?

STEVE:
Precisely. Take your first chapter, for example. The story is set in the first person, and yet your hero, Briggs, walks into a bar, a dimly-lit bar, and straightaway notices some odd details, even for a Private Eye with twenty-twenty.

TONY:
Like what?

STEVE:
For starters, the way he describes the guy at the end of the room, the biker he's been tracking down . . .

TONY:
Hackett.

STEVE:
Right, Hackett . . . Now Briggs is — what? — thirty feet away from Hackett in this smoke-filled bar, yet Briggs describes Hackett's blue-grey eyes, the diamond stud in his left earlobe, the tiny scar on his chin. However, it's not till Briggs takes a few steps into the room that his eyesight becomes truly paranormal. That's when he notices a loose thread on the third button of Hackett's shirt. He even notices the threads a different colour and a different stitch.

TONY:
Alright, alright. I get the point.

PAM:
Only describe what the narrator can plausibly see for himself.

STEVE:
That's right. Otherwise, the reader might hurl the book at the wall. Or worse, not buy your next one.

TONY:

Now I understand why I'm giving lube jobs and you're giving interviews. Anyway, thanks Steve. I appreciate the good advice . . . Oh, by the way, there is something else I wanted to ask you. Do you think it's possible I could get paid for that job I did for you? I kind of need the money.

STEVE:

I see. So you didn't brave the storm just to get my literary critique. And here I was congratulating us both: You for your dedication, and me as the writer who inspired it . . .   *(He crosses to the desk)*   Alright, but I'll have to pay you by cheque, Tony. I don't have much cash on me . . .   *(He gets out his chequebook)*

TONY:

A cheque's fine. Make it out to Harry's Autobody, would you? He's threatened to fire me unless I pay him the three hundred dollars I lost on a bet. I figure the work I did for you was worth at least three hundred, don't you? Considering the nature of the job, and all? . . .
(STEVE gives him a look and begins writing out the cheque)

PAM:

Tell me, Tony. Exactly what sort of work did you do for my husband? I thought the car had already been fixed?

TONY:

No, it wasn't the car, Mrs. Marsh. It was just . . . You know, carpentry work. That sort of thing.

PAM:

Carpentry work? I don't recall any repairs being done to the house.

STEVE:
It wasn't here, it was up at the cottage. Remember last
summer you complained about the neighbours? How
their dog kept digging up the flower bed? Well, that
won't happen again. Tony and I drove up there one day
last week and fenced in the yard.

PAM:
Fenced in the yard? Really?

STEVE:
We also tilled the garden and planted flowers.
Impatiens. Asters. Petunias . . . What else? Oh, yes. Your
favorite: snapdragons . . .   *(He rips off the cheque and
hands it to TONY)*   There. And tell Harry if he ever
fires you, I'm taking my business elsewhere. Okay?

TONY:
Thanks, Steve, you're a lifesaver. Goodnight, Mrs.
Marsh. It was nice meeting you.

PAM:
It was nice meeting you too, Tony . . . Let me show you
out.

TONY:
Don't bother, I know the way . . .   *(He turns just before
he exits the room)*   You know, Steve, something just
occurred to me. About the fence, I mean. I just wonder
if it'll keep out smaller animals. Skunks like to dig up
gardens, don't they? So do raccoons . . .

STEVE:
Point taken. I suppose I'll have to keep an eye on that,
won't I? Just in case. Goodnight, now.

TONY exits. Sound of thunder.

PAM:
It's a wonder he didn't forget his story. You suppose
he'll lose all interest in it now he's been told he might
have to rewrite?

STEVE:
I thought he took the criticism quite well. A lot better
than most would at his age.

PAM:
He's a strange one, though, isn't he? What was he in jail
for? Did he say?

STEVE:
Auto theft. Burglary.

PAM:
Burglary? No wonder he was peeking in the window, it's
probably second nature to him.

STEVE:
Oh, come on. Anyone who's been in prison is bound to
appear strange. The truth is he's harmless.

PAM:
I'm not so sure. You weren't in the room when he was
describing that movie, *The Spiral Staircase.* I had the
distinct impression he was trying to frighten me.

STEVE:
That's just Tony. He's so crazy about the mystery genre,
he gets carried away sometimes.   *(He crosses to the
bookcase and searches for something to read)*

PAM:
What's going on, Steven? I find it odd you'd hire Tony
and not tell me. That fence must've been expensive,

wasn't it? And you know we talked about selling the property . . .

STEVE:
> I know we did. But Pam, you know how much I love that place. As much as your father did. I can't stand the thought of selling it any more than he could . . .

> *Doorbell.*

STEVE:
> That'll be Tony. Want to bet he couldn't get his bike to start?

PAM:
> Either that, or he's decided to mug us both and be done with it . . .   *(She exits into the hall)*

> *STEVE returns to his computer. PAM appears in the doorway. She looks troubled.*

STEVE: *(rising)*
> What is it? What's the matter?

PAM:
> It isn't Tony . . .

STEVE:
> Oh? Who is it?   *(Then)*   Pam?

PAM:
> You have a visitor. She says she's looking for her sister. She thinks you might have knowledge of her where- abouts . . .

STEVE:
> Really?

PAM:

Steven, she says her sister is Christine Dodd. That's the young woman who interviewed you, isn't it?

> *GEMMA DODD appears in the doorway. There is something austere about GEMMA, almost daunting, as though she cared little about the values of the modern world. Unlike her sister, GEMMA wears little makeup and no jewellery. She is perhaps two years younger than her sister, a striking brunette with shoulder length hair. She wears a trenchcoat buckled at the waist, and speaks with an English accent.*

GEMMA:

Hi, Steve. Long time, no see . . .

STEVE:

Hello Gemma . . . What's this I hear about Chris? My wife says she's missing.

GEMMA:

Yes. Almost a week now . . . Look, I realize it's late, Steve, but I need to talk to you. If your wife wouldn't mind, that is.

PAM:

Actually, I would mind. Anything that needs to be said to my husband can be said in front of me. I don't think that's unreasonable.

GEMMA:

Very well. I just thought . . .

PAM:

What's going on, Steven? I've never heard you mention this woman. Was there something between you and her sister? Is that it?

STEVE:

No, that's not it. Oh, God, the truth is I'm in a no-win situation. No matter how I explain this, I'll only come off looking bad.

PAM:

Explain what?

STEVE:

Remember that day Christine was here? Well, I allowed her to play a prank. A juvenile prank.

PAM:

What sort of prank?

STEVE:

The so-called interview. Chris doesn't write for magazines, she's an actress. She had a small part in *Hangman's Noose.* That's how I met her and Gemma.

PAM:

An actress? . . .

STEVE:

The ruse seemed innocent enough at the time. That's why I went along with it. Not that I'm excusing myself . . . It's no mystery why she came here. She's moving to the States. To get her Green Card, she needs letters of recommendation.

GEMMA:

That's why she was here that day? To get a letter for American Immigration?

STEVE:

That's right. I told her I'd be only too happy to oblige. In fact, I wrote her the letter while she looked through an old *National Geographic.*

GEMMA:

And you haven't seen her since?

STEVE:

No. Why would I? Chris and I are not exactly friends,
are we? I doubt if I'll ever hear from her again.

GEMMA:

That's not the truth. He knows a great deal more than
he's letting on. But I'll get to that later . . . You see, I
think something's happened to Chris. It's not just the
fact she hasn't been in touch. It's more than that . . .

PAM:
Oh?

GEMMA:

Three days ago I flew back from Zurich. I work for Air
Canada, I'm a flight attendant . . . Chris and I share a
house together. Near the Summerhill tube . . . It was
eerie. As soon as I stepped in the door, I had the
strangest feeling. As though something had happened
there recently . . .

PAM:

Why? Are you and your sister close?

GEMMA:

Not really. Most of our lives we've been separated. Chris
lived here with my father, and I lived with my mother in
England.

STEVE:

Let me get this straight, Gemma. You think Chris has
come to some harm because you arrived back from
Zurich and felt uneasy? My God, did it ever occur to

you that what you experienced might simply be jet lag
or culture shock?

PAM:
Be serious, Steve.

STEVE:
I am serious. For all you know, she might be shacked up
somewhere. She may even have gotten a film out of
town.

GEMMA:
I called her agent. He hasn't heard from her in over a
week . . . No, it's just not like Chris to stay away like this.
Not without letting me know. Besides, there was something else . . .

PAM:
What?

GEMMA:
I think our house has been burgled. It must've
happened while I was away.

PAM:
Burgled? Are you sure?

GEMMA:
At first I thought it was just Chris. You know, maybe
she'd gone through my dresser, looking for something
to wear.

PAM: (uneasily)
Yes, I'm sure that's all it was . . .   (She glances at
STEVE)

GEMMA:

Then I began to wonder. I noticed other things out of place. In the living room . . . the kitchen. Even the bathroom. As though someone had searched the house and not quite put things back the way they were. I couldn't prove it, of course. Not until tonight. That's when I found this . . . *(She produces a tape cassette from the pocket of her trenchcoat)*

PAM:

What is it?

GEMMA:

Mahler. Gustav Mahler. At least that's what Chris had scribbled on it . . . Imagine my surprise, Steve. There I was rummaging through our tapes and what did I find but Mahler's Fourth. Chris is no great fan of classical music, so I thought it strange she'd tape it.

STEVE:

What's your point?

GEMMA:

I think you already know. It turns out Mahler isn't Mahler at all. In fact, the only thing on the tape is a conversation between you and my sister. A conversation that apparently took place on the day she came here to interview you.

PAM:

She did have a tape recorder, Steven. You even commented on it, remember?

GEMMA:

My first impulse was to go to the Police. But I realized if I did that, and Chris suddenly popped up, the tape could prove her guilty of blackmail. That's why I

64

decided to come here first. Just to hear what you had to say.

PAM:

Her sister was blackmailing you?

STEVE:

Look, let's discuss this later, shall we? Now is hardly the time.

PAM:

Answer me, dammit. What exactly did she have on you? What?

STEVE:

Later, Pamela.

PAM:

Not later. Now.

STEVE:

Alright. I was supposed to pay her a large sum of money. Fifty thousand dollars. In exchange for which, she'd keep quiet about the affair.

PAM:

Affair? What affair? You said you weren't involved with that girl.

STEVE:

I wasn't. The affair was with Gemma, not Chris. With Gemma.

PAM:

Gemma? I see . . .

STEVE:
I'm sorry.

PAM:
That's it? You're sorry?! . . . *(She slaps his face)*
That's for putting me through hell. That's for making
me doubt myself. Oh, you are one sick man, Steven.
One real sonofabitch.

STEVE:
Look, I don't expect forgiveness. I don't even expect
you to understand. I had an affair, and I'm sorry. I
made a mistake, alright?

PAM:
A mistake?!

STEVE:
That's right. Not everyone's perfect, you know. You
don't think I'm ashamed of what I did? You don't think
I'm devastated? And if I lied to you, Pamela, it's because
I knew what would happen if I told you the truth. I was
desperate.

GEMMA:
And desperate people do desperate things, don't they?
You know what I think happened, Steve? I think you
broke into our house, looking for the tape. Only my
sister outsmarted you by leaving the tape right out in
the open.

STEVE:
Listen. I wouldn't burgle a house if a movie deal
depended on it. For one thing, I don't have the nerve.

GEMMA:
Maybe not. But if Chris isn't home soon, I'm going to the Police. I'll let them decide if you had anything to do with the break-in.

Thunder. Lightning.

STEVE:
I'm sorry, Gemma. I can't let you give the Police that tape. You know that, don't you? . . .   *(He starts towards her)*   So give it to me.

GEMMA: *(backing away)*
No. Keep away.

STEVE:
Come on, now, Gemma. Give me the tape. Don't make me use force.

PAM:
Steven . . .

STEVE:
I'm surprised you came here tonight. You really shouldn't have, you know. That's not very smart. Bringing the tape along with you . . .

PAM:
Steven, stop it. I mean it. This is beginning to frighten me.

STEVE:
Stay out of it, Pamela. Gemma should understand I can't let her keep it. Now hand it over, Gemma, and you won't get hurt. I promise.

GEMMA backs up to the coffee table. She notices the silver dagger. Snatching it up, she brandishes the dagger.

GEMMA:
I'm warning you, Steve. Stay away from me. Don't come any closer.

PAM:
Leave her alone, Steven. What do you care about the tape? It can't be used to blackmail you now.

STEVE:
What if she's right, Pam? What if something's happened to Chris? If that's the case, then the tape provides me with a perfect motive for murder.

GEMMA:
Murder?

PAM:
No one mentioned murder, Steven . . .

STEVE:
Pam, they'll think I killed her because she was black-mailing me. Don't you see, I could be implicated in her death simply because of some bloody tape.

GEMMA:
My God, he's killed Christine. I know it. That's why he can't let the tape fall into the wrong hands. Not because he's innocent, but because he's guilty!

STEVE lunges at GEMMA. She swipes at him with the dagger, but he manages to seize her wrists, making her drop it to the floor.

PAM:

Steven, stop it! Let her alone! Steven!

GEMMA kicks him in the groin and rushes for the French doors. She grabs a steel-tipped walking stick from the umbrella stand and smashes STEVE across the head. He drops to his knees, dazed. GEMMA throws open the drapes and unbolts the French doors. STEVE rouses himself and snatches up the dagger from the floor.

PAM:

Steven! No! Don't! No!

GEMMA rushes out the French doors, but STEVE pursues her. Through the windows, we watch as STEVE stabs her twice. Lightning flashes, not only punctuating the murder, but allowing us to see it . . . PAM freezes, moaning . . . STEVE returns to the room, clutching the dagger, his shirt wet with rain and splattered with blood. He, too, seems to be in shock. Suddenly he becomes aware of the dagger in his hand and drops it to the floor, frightened . . .

PAM:

Dear God, what have you done? Look at yourself, Steven! Look! . . .

STEVE:

Shut up. Let me think, will you? We have to remain calm . . .

PAM:

What happened to her sister? She's dead, too, isn't she? Which one of you did it?

STEVE:

Tony never meant to harm her. It was an accident. She walked in on him. He tried to stop her from screaming . . .

PAM:

> She's buried at the cottage, isn't she? That's why you and Tony were there. That's why you fenced in the yard . . . My God, what have you done? This could destroy our lives.

STEVE:

> Not if we don't call the Police.

PAM:

> What?

STEVE:

> No one needs to know. Tony and I got rid of Chris' body, didn't we? I can get rid of Gemma's the same way . . . *(He exits into the garden and returns with the tape cassette, which he tosses on his desk)* Now there's nothing to connect me to Gemma. In any case, I have an alibi. 'I was at the theatre, Inspector. My wife and I went straight home to bed. You can ask her yourself.'

PAM:

> What kind of man are you, Steven? You just killed someone. Someone you knew intimately. Don't you feel anything? Not even remorse?

STEVE:

> Apparently not. Frankly, the only feeling I have right now is an urge to clean up the mess I've made. I take it that makes me a pragmatist.

PAM:

> She couldn't be allowed to leave here alive, could she? You knew that from the moment she showed you the tape. Isn't that right? Isn't it?

STEVE:

Alright, call the Police. Go on, I'll help you . . . *(He picks up the handset and holds it out to her)* The press will love it, won't they? 'MYSTERY WRITER HIRES EX-CON.' 'WRITER SLAYS LOVER IN FRONT OF WIFE.' Adultery . . . blackmail . . . murder. And what a cast of characters: Award-winning author . . . film actress . . . flight attendant . . . ex-con. And last but not least, Pamela Marsh. 'PROFESSOR OF CRIME FICTION INVOLVED IN MURDER.' Oh, your colleagues will eat it up, won't they? Especially the Dean and your department head. Not to mention the members of the promotion committee.

PAM:

You bastard.

STEVE:

Now, now. I'm just pointing out the error of your ways. Especially considering whose daughter you are. You don't want the press drooling over that, do you? Dragging your father's name through the mud? . . . *(PAM turns away)* Now why don't you go on upstairs? I'll take care of things down here.

PAM:

Do you really think I could stay in this house tonight? After what's happened? No, I'll stay at a hotel.

STEVE:

Suit yourself.

PAM:

I'm selling the house, Steven. As soon as the estate is settled. I want a divorce.

STEVE:

Selling the house?

PAM:

That's right. I can't imagine living with you now. I want you out of my life as soon as possible. You understand?

STEVE:

I wouldn't mention divorce if I were you. Not until you've got your promotion. Then if you still feel the same way, we can discuss it.

PAM:

There's nothing to discuss, Steven. You take from our marriage what you brought to it. That means your freedom and nothing else.

STEVE:

Let's talk about this another time, shall we? Right now you're blinded by emotion. I don't think you see the bind you're in.

PAM:

Bind? What bind?

STEVE:

Think about it. If you call the Police, the scandal will ruin you. If you don't call, you become guilty of concealing murder. Either way, you lose.

PAM:

We'll see who loses.

STEVE:

Oh, don't worry, Pam, I'll agree to divorce. But on my own terms, not your father's.

PAM:
Tell me something, Steven. Did you ever feel anything for me? Or was it all a sham? All pretense? No, spare me the lie, I think I know . . . *(She exits into the hall. A moment later, we see her putting on her coat. Then we hear the front door slam behind her)*

STEVE:
I think you always knew what I was like, Pam. You just refused to believe it.

Lightning flashes. STEVE picks up the dagger from the floor, takes out his handkerchief, and wipes the blade clean. As he is doing this, GEMMA begins to crawl slowly into the room, her face and clothes wet and bloody. Lightning flashes again. She pulls herself to her feet, takes the steel letter-opener from the desk, and slowly approaches STEVE from behind. With both hands on the hilt, she raises the letter-opener as if to plunge it into STEVE's back —

STEVE:
Don't do that, Chris. You'll frighten me . . . *(He sets the Silver Dagger back on its stand)*

CHRIS: *(dropping the accent)*
God, it was just like opening night, wasn't it? The whole thing worked like a charm. *(She whips off her wig and tosses it on the desk)*

STEVE: *(takes the letter-opener from her and sets it on the desk)*
Of course it worked. Like a good mystery it was carefully thought out. Down to the last detail. Did you ever doubt we'd pull it off?

CHRIS: *(pours herself a drink at the buffet)*
Only when you first suggested the idea. However, the promise of seventy-five grand soon restored my faith . . .

My God, that blood pack is effective, isn't it? And that was a great idea, Steve, to give Gemma an English accent.

Lightning flashes as TONY enters the French doors.

TONY:
Man, oh man, what a night. Even the weather was on our side.　　*(He closes the French doors and peels off his raincoat)*

STEVE:
I thought we were all very convincing. The husband with a guilty conscience . . . the ex-con hired to build a fence . . . the distraught sister . . .　　*(He tosses the tape cassette to CHRIS)*　　I take it this isn't the real tape?

CHRIS:
Of course it is. You don't think I'd be dumb enough not to bring the real one, do you? What if she'd wanted to listen to it?

STEVE:
I thought it might be a copy.

CHRIS:
The cat's out of the bag. Why make a copy?

STEVE pours a drink for TONY and himself.

TONY:
Hey, Steve, I gotta hand it to you. It's like you said. If you're going to lie, stick close to the truth. Then you don't have to invent too much.

STEVE:　　*(hands TONY his drink)*
I also said to stick to the script, Tony. Do you realize you almost gave the whole thing away, you putz?

TONY:
I did? How?

STEVE:
That stuff you tossed in about *The Spiral Staircase.* I
warned you my wife was no fool. She sensed you were
trying to frighten her.

TONY:
That's not what I was doing, Steve. It was more like
foreshadowing . . .

STEVE:
Then you have to be more subtle, Tony. That was far
too obvious.

TONY:
Obvious? I'll tell you what's obvious, Steve. Obvious is
making the first chapter of my book into the work of
some friggin' amateur. I was offended!

STEVE:
Don't be so sensitive. It was all part of the scam.

TONY:
So what? I know there are writers who make these kind
of mistakes, but I don't want to be lumped in with
them. What? Do I look like an idiot? 'He even notices
the threads a different colour and a different stitch.'
Christ, I was so embarrassed I almost confessed.

*Lightning flashes twice, freezing the room in a ghostly
tableau. Thunder rolls down the sky into the —*

Blackout.

ACT TWO

SCENE ONE

A week later. It is a lovely afternoon, with the French doors wide open.

The Silver Dagger is now on the mantle. A coffee service is on the coffee table.

At rise, STEVE is hard at work on his fourth novel, the keys of the word processor making a soft click. PAM stands at a distance, flipping through the pages of a newspaper. Two suitcases stand in the hall at the bottom of the stairs.

PAM:
You'd think by now someone would have reported them missing.

STEVE: *(tapping away)*
It's only been a week or so. Besides, why would it make the papers unless the Police suspect foul play?   *(He stops writing, studies her)*   Actually, this conference couldn't have come at a better time. It'll do you good to get away.

PAM:
Do me good? I can't get that night out of my mind. Why haven't you gotten rid of that knife?

STEVE:
What? My Silver Dagger?

PAM:
It's a murder weapon now, Steven, not an award.

STEVE:

I don't care what it is, I'm not pitching it out. Christ, it's a symbol of artistic respect. *(He rises, stretches)*

PAM:

That symbol could land you in prison. Both of us, for that matter. And believe me, that's an even bleaker place than the blank page . . . *(Glances at her watch)* I wish Jane would hurry. The limo's going to be here soon.

STEVE:

Listen, no one's going to connect us to Chris or Gemma. But suppose they do? Do you really believe they'll cart my Silver Dagger off to Forensics?

PAM:

The Police are not stupid, Steven.

STEVE:

I'm not saying they are. I'm saying I won that award as runner-up for the best crime novel of the year, and I'm not about to chuck it down the drain. Besides, Tony would have a stroke.

PAM:

Has he predicted *Natural Causes* will win the Gold Dagger this year?

STEVE:

Not only that, he swears it'll take the Edgar. Plus make the New York Times Bestseller List.

PAM:

It's pathetic the way he flatters you. Even more pathetic is the way you eat it up.

STEVE:

Give me some credit, will you? Having your ego stroked is like sex. You don't have to take it seriously just because you like it.

Doorbell.

STEVE:

I'll get that. I'm going to fix myself some lunch. *(He starts out of the room)* By the way, did you remember your passport?

PAM looks away.

STEVE:

No, I didn't think so. Never mind, I'll get it.

STEVE exits into the hall. Off, we hear him let JANE in. Then STEVE goes upstairs. JANE enters the library, carrying her briefcase.

JANE:

Hi, you.

PAM:

What kept you? Busy day?

JANE:

Sorry for cutting it so close. Yes, I have an old friend in Toronto General. He's having major surgery in the morning and wanted to go over his will. Just in case . . . *(She sets down her briefcase)* How I envy you the Caribbean. All that white sand. How long will you be gone?

PAM:

Two weeks . . . Coffee?

JANE:
   Please.

PAM: *(pouring the coffee)*
   Frankly, I wish I didn't have to give the paper. I'd sooner
   sit under a beach umbrella with the latest James Lee
   Burke . . .   *(Hands JANE her coffee)*

JANE:
   Are you alright? You look tired. You haven't been
   getting more of those letters, have you?

PAM:
   No, they've stopped. So have the phone calls.

JANE:
   I've been giving it some thought. You don't suppose it
   might be someone from your department? Someone
   who's being passed over?

PAM:
   That's what Steven thinks. Anyway, I was wrong about
   him, wrong about the affair. But look, I didn't drag you
   here to discuss all that. What I want to talk about is our
   Marriage Contract.

JANE:
   Oh?

PAM:
   It's been on my mind all week. The fact is, the more I
   think about it, the more unfair it seems to Steven.

JANE:
   Is that your word or his? Because the Pre-nuptial was
   meant to protect you, not your husband.

PAM:

The Pre-nuptial was my father's idea. Well, I'm independent now. As of today, I want my husband to be an equal in this marriage, not a junior partner.

JANE:

I understand how you feel. But as your lawyer, I don't like it. I mean, it was only two weeks ago you stood in this room and declared yourself all for it.

PAM:

A lot can happen in two weeks.

JANE:

What? A complete about-face?

PAM:

Look, I don't want to discuss this any further. As far as I'm concerned, I've made it abundantly clear what I want.

JANE:

Alright, I'll shred the contract as soon as I have it in writing. But I still think you're making a big mistake . . . *(Picks up her briefcase)* Is that it for the day? Because if there's nothing else . . .

PAM:

Wait, wait . . . Actually, Jane, there is something else. Only I just don't know where to begin . . . *(STEVE appears on the landing, PAM's passport in his hand. He listens)* . . . Let me ask you this: a lawyer can't reveal what her client has told her, can she? Even if the client admits to witnessing a crime?

JANE:

That's right. Not only that, the client is under no legal obligation to report the crime.

PAM:

Not even homicide?

JANE:

Not even homicide. Naturally, I'd advise her she has a
civic and moral duty to contact the Police. But she
couldn't be charged with anything. Not unless she were
an accessory to the crime, or an accomplice.

PAM:

What's the difference?

JANE:

Let's say you drove the getaway car in a bank robbery.
That would make you an accomplice. But if you only
hid the car for the robber, that would make you an
accessory. Failing to report a crime doesn't make you
either an accomplice or an accessory.

PAM:

I see . . .

JANE:

Now are you going to tell me what this is all about?
Exactly what sort of crime did you witness?

STEVE: *(entering)*

What else, my dear Watson? Murder most foul.

JANE:

Murder?

PAM:

You were eavesdropping, Steven.

STEVE:

Actually, love, I was fetching your passport. I admit I did
catch the tailend of your conversation. I'm not entirely

deaf . . .   *(Hands PAM the passport)*   You'll have to forgive her, Jane. Pam's not been herself lately. In fact, you'll never believe who the murderer is. Go on, Pam. Tell her.   *(Then)*   Go on. Don't be shy.

PAM:
It's Steven.

JANE:
Steven?

STEVE:
Have you ever heard anything more preposterous? She's obviously had a dream so vivid she's convinced herself it was real. She's convinced I murdered a woman in cold blood.

PAM:
You did, Steven.

STEVE:
Don't talk rubbish. I'm no more a killer than you are. The only murder I'm capable of is in my books.

PAM:
He stabbed her to death the night of that storm. He chased her into the garden. I watched him do it.

JANE:
Who was this woman?

STEVE:
Apparently she was an old lover of mine. Is that right, Pam? And I stabbed her to death — this is the best part — with the award I won from the British Crime Writers. *(Picks up the dagger)*   This Silver Dagger.

JANE:
Pam?

PAM: *(to JANE)*
Don't you see what he's trying to do? He's very good at
turning things around . . . Yes, he stabbed her. I already
told you that. He stabbed her twice. I saw the blood. It
was on his shirt . . .

STEVE:
Absurd. Don't you remember, that's why I had to leave
med. school? The sight of blood makes me faint. Are
you going to pretend I just made that up?

PAM walks upstage, genuinely puzzled.

STEVE:
Pam's under a great deal of stress. Her father's death.
Those letters and phone calls . . . her book . . . her
paper . . . the promotion.

PAM:
He's lying, I tell you. I saw him kill that woman. I know I
did. I didn't imagine it. I didn't dream it. It was real.

STEVE:
Real? Pam, I couldn't use that dagger in a murder
mystery, and you know it. The reader wouldn't stand for
it.

PAM:
He'd say anything to protect himself, can't you see that?
Anything to discredit me.

STEVE:
What would you have me do, love? Confess to murder
just to appease you? The truth is I've killed no one, in
spite of what you claim to have seen. No one.

JANE: (*examining the dagger*)
Pam, are you sure about this? I just can't . . .

PAM:
What are you saying, Jane? That you don't believe me?
If that's the case, say it. Go on.

JANE:
That's not what I meant, Pam. So don't put words in
my mouth. It's just that you've made a very serious
charge . . .

PAM:
I don't believe this. Now my best friend is turning
against me.   *(To JANE)*   You don't even know
you're being manipulated , do you?

JANE:
I wish you wouldn't do that. I'm not taking sides in this.
I'm simply trying to understand.

PAM:
No, you were implying that I better be damn certain I'm
not accusing an innocent man. Steven's planted doubt
in your mind, hasn't he? Has he also made you suspect
my mental state? Has he?

JANE:
No, Pam, he hasn't. If anyone's done that, it's you, not
Steven. The last time I was here you said you wanted to
keep the Pre-nuptial. Today you ordered me to shred it.
And why? Because you're concerned that Steven be
treated fairly. Yet a minute later, you accuse him of
murder . . .

PAM:
I get it. I'm just a garden variety mental case. Maybe
bordering on delusional. Is that it, Jane? . . . Well,

goodbye. Thanks for the vote of confidence. That'll be all for today.

JANE:

Look, Pam . . .

PAM:

Goodbye, I said. I know you're busy, and I've got a plane to catch. Steven will show you to the door.

JANE: *(picks up her briefcase)*

That won't be necessary, Steve. Thanks all the same, but I can find my own way out. *(She exits)*

STEVE:

That was pretty childish, wasn't it? It's hardly Jane's fault she doesn't believe you.

PAM:

Now you listen to me, Steven. I learned an interesting fact today. Failing to report a crime doesn't make me a criminal. That means I can't be charged with anything. Understand?

STEVE:

Don't be tiresome, Pam. You know you're too ambitious to turn me in. Besides, you'd better pray I'm never charged with Gemma's murder. Because if I am, I'll simply say it was you who did it.

PAM:

Me? I didn't kill her, you did.

STEVE:

Did I? I could make a perfectly good case why you stabbed Gemma. Would you like to hear it? 'It's this way, Inspector. Miss Dodd and I were former lovers, and when she came here that night looking for her sister, my wife discovered the affair and stabbed her in a fit of jealous rage. I'm sure you've heard what my wife is like, Inspector.'

PAM:
No one would believe that, least of all the Police.

STEVE:
Wouldn't they? Remember the girl you tossed your wine at? She'd make a strong impression on the witness stand. 'She hurled her drink in my face, your Honour, all because of a piece of lint.'

PAM:
You know, Steven, you're not always going to come up a winner. One of these days I'm going to pay you back. That I promise you.   *(She exits upstairs)*

STEVE:
Rule Number One, Pam. Never make promises you can't keep. Ah, Tony . . .

At that moment, TONY runs in through the French doors. He is dressed in blue jeans and sneakers, with a T-shirt and red polka dot headband. Slightly out of breath, he drops to his knees.

TONY:
Oh, wow. Man, oh, man . . . Steve, I gotta quit smoking two packs a day. Even my Parole Officer runs faster.

STEVE:
I didn't know you jogged, Tony. You never struck me as the masochistic type.

TONY:
Who's been jogging? Some friggin' dog just chased me up the block. Almost bit my ass off. At least I got a

sentence out of it. Listen to this: 'The German shepherd gave a short, almost tentative howl, like a lick on a badly-played trumpet.' What do you think?

Doorbell.

STEVE:
That's the limo . . .

TONY:
Of a badly played trumpet?

STEVE: *(crosses into the hall and yells up the stairs)*
Pam, the car's here! I'll take your luggage out!

TONY:
You want a hand, Steve?

STEVE:
No, I can manage . . .   *(He picks up the two suitcases and exits)*

> *PAM comes hurrying down the stairs, clutching her purse. She notices TONY in the library and enters.*

PAM:
I know what you did to that young actress, Tony.

TONY:
Yes, Ma'am.

PAM:
If you know what's good for you, you'll have nothing more to do with Steven.

TONY:
Really?

PAM:
    He's not what he appears to be.   *(She rushes off)*

TONY:
    Whew! That was like Ethel Barrymore in *The Spiral
    Staircase*. 'Leave this house tonight — if you know what's
    good for you.' . . .   *(He wanders over to the word
    processor, glances at the screen, then reads aloud)*   'The
    morgue was a small, squat stucco building. Unless you
    knew the town of Elroy, Sharpe thought, it could easily
    be mistaken for the local library . . . '

    *At that moment, STEVE returns, exploding into sudden
    fury..*

STEVE:
    What the hell are you doing? ! Did I say you could read
    my work? Did I? That's like sifting through my dirty
    laundry.

TONY:
    Your dirty laundry?

STEVE:
    Not even Pam reads my rough work. Not Pam, not my
    editor, and especially not you. Understand?

TONY:
    Hey, I'm sorry, I . . .

STEVE:
    What do you do for kicks, Tony? Peep in windows at
    night? Bore holes through walls? Listen with a glass to
    your ear? Christ, now I have to toss out a whole day's
    work. How much did you read?

TONY:
Hardly any. A sentence or two.

STEVE:
Don't lie to me, dammit.

TONY:
Alright, I read the first paragraph. Which by the way is terrific. Especially the last sentence. 'And then the rain fell, rattling on the hood of Sharpe's red Honda.'

STEVE: *(relenting slightly)*
You like that, do you?

TONY:
Like it? What's not to like? Those r's sound like raindrops rattling on the tin frame of the car. Only a pro can do that, Steve. A master at the peak of his powers.

STEVE:
If only I wasn't so modest, I might be tempted to agree.

TONY:
I'll tell you something else, Steve. It's just a hunch I have . . . a sort of premonition . . . but this book could do for you what *The Thin Man* did for Dashiell Hammett.

STEVE:
Let's hope not, Tony. *The Thin Man* was the last novel Dashiell Hammett ever wrote. You mean *The Maltese Falcon*, don't you? . . .

The phone rings. STEVE answers it.

STEVE:
Hello . . . Yes, I have . . . No, she just left . . . Fine. Park in the driveway . . .   *(He hangs up)*

TONY:
> Christine?

STEVE:
> She's up at the corner. Look, we still have a minute or two. Is there anything you want to go over? Anything you're not sure of?

TONY:
> No. We rehearsed it enough . . . I still don't like it, though. She's no dummy, Steve. What if it doesn't work?

STEVE:
> Trust me: It'll work.

TONY:
> I know it'll work. But what if it doesn't?

STEVE:
> In that case, we'll have to eliminate her some other way.

TONY:
> What do you mean, 'eliminate'? That's the trouble, Steve, I never know when you're being serious . . .

STEVE:
> Besides, I'm not letting some two-bit blackmailer get her hooks in me. You don't really think I'd give her seventy-five grand, do you? As soon as that ran out, she'd be back for more. Guaranteed.

TONY:
> Alright, but count me out. No way do I want to go back to the slammer. Not on a charge of first degree murder. No way, José

STEVE:

Relax. It won't come to that. I promise.

TONY:

Then why do I have such a strong sense of foreboding?

STEVE:

Look, what do you think I'm going to do? Pull a fast
one? . . . God, I'm surprised at you, Tony. I thought you
were a better judge of character than that.   *(He
crosses to the desk and removes the gun from its drawer)*
Come on, look, they're blanks. So no one gets hurt . . .
*(He offers the gun to TONY, but TONY shrugs it off. STEVE
puts the gun back in the drawer)*   Now did you strap on
the blood pack?

TONY:

All set.

STEVE:

Good. And remember, try to fall on the area rug. I
don't want the carpet stained.

      Doorbell.

STEVE:

That's it. Curtain up . . .   *(He exits into the hall)*

      *TONY hurries out the French doors, closing them behind
      him. STEVE ushers CHRIS into the library. She is
      wearing a summer dress and sandals. Over her shoulder,
      she carries a purse. (Note: this is the first time we see the
      real CHRIS, since in both her other scenes she was playing
      a 'character' and therefore somewhat made up for the part)*

CHRIS:

Funny, isn't it? You'd think someone as smart as Pam would have caught on. Then again, she thinks she's too smart to be fooled.

STEVE:

She finds it odd no one's reported you or Gemma missing. Especially Gemma. She's supposed to be a flight attendant. Those sort of people live more structured lives.

CHRIS:

Listen, you're the writer. I don't have to tell you how to cover your tracks. It shouldn't be hard to explain why two women have disappeared.

STEVE:

No, you're right. Anyone can disappear. It happens all the time . . .   *(He crosses to the buffet and pours himself a Scotch)*

CHRIS:

By the way, you'll never guess what I read this week? *Natural Causes.* All two hundred and eighty pages. It's your best yet, Steve.

STEVE:

I like it.

CHRIS:

I think it would make a great film, don't you? It's so cinematic. And you know the part I'd kill for? The femme fatal. She's so beautifully written.

STEVE:

What are you getting at?

CHRIS:

Just that I was born to play Tonya. Steve, I know her.
The way you describe her, it could be me. It's almost as
if you modeled her on me.

STEVE:

Well, I didn't. And even if I had, I'd never admit it.

CHRIS:

I'll tell you what else I did. I mentioned it to my agent.
He thinks I'd be wise to take an option on the novel
and get you to write the screenplay. You think we could
reach an agreement?

STEVE:

A screenplay? Get serious, will you?

CHRIS:

Steve, you did a terrific job on *Hangman's Noose*. And
this way you wouldn't have to fret about some screen-
writer butchering your book, you could do it yourself.

STEVE:

Very funny.

CHRIS:

The timing's perfect. I'll be in L.A. soon, I can pitch it.
And don't tell me you wouldn't mind Hollywood
filming one of your novels. Nick Nolte as Inspector
Sharpe. Donald Sutherland as Nash.

STEVE:

Introducing Christine Dodd. I get it.

CHRIS:

We'd keep the story line, and the characters. All you'd
have to change is the setting. Make it New York, maybe.
Or San Francisco.

STEVE:

There's just one flaw in your scenario. No Hollywood producer would trust an unknown with the role of Tonya. You know it, and I know it.

CHRIS:

That depends on how badly they want the property, and who owns it. That's why I need the film rights.

STEVE:

You expect me to let some bit player tie up the film rights to the most commercial novel I've ever written? You must be out of your mind.

CHRIS:

What are you saying, Steve? That you don't think I could put the package together? You know what I'm like when I put my mind to something.

STEVE:

Yes. The same way I know you'll bleed me dry, drop by drop . . .   *(He crosses to the desk. From the drawer he removes the gun, making sure CHRIS sees it. He then takes out a white envelope)*   Here. The down payment. Fifteen thousand in large currency. Just the way you wanted. *(Hands it to CHRIS)*   Count it.

CHRIS:

Not that I don't trust you . . .   *(She sits and begins to count the bills)*

> *Meanwhile, STEVE puts the gun back in the drawer. He closes the French doors, then draws the drapes . . . Suddenly CHRIS becomes aware of what he's just done. Maybe it's the change of light that makes her look up. Or some intuitive sense of her own danger.*

STEVE: *(switching on the table lamp)*
I was just thinking, Chris. There is a simple explanation
why someone like you might disappear. It's so obvious it
never occurred to me.

CHRIS:
What is it?

STEVE:
Hollywood.

CHRIS:
Hollywood?

STEVE:
Sure. Millions of kids flock there every year, don't they?
Most never make it in films. Some are never heard from
again. That's a fact of life, isn't it?

CHRIS:
What if it is? . . .

STEVE:
They fall through the cracks in the American Dream
and vanish. Girls like you. Some with talent. Some
whose luck just runs out.   *(He snaps his fingers. TONY
slips into the library from the hall. He stands blocking the
doorway)*

CHRIS:
What is this, Steve? Some sort of double cross? . . . I
thought we had a deal?

STEVE:
Sorry, love. All deals are off.

The switchblade appears in TONY's hand. The blade snaps open.

CHRIS:

What's going on, Steve? Whatever it is, you're making a big mistake. You won't get away with it.

STEVE:

You think not?

CHRIS:

If you're trying to scare me, okay, you succeeded. I'm scared. Now what? . . . You want the money back? Okay, just take it. It's yours . . . *(She drops it on the coffee table)* Just tell Tony to put down that knife, alright?

STEVE:

Did you really think I'd sit still for a shakedown? First, it was money you wanted. Now it's my work. *(He nods to TONY. From this moment on, TONY moves menacingly toward CHRIS)*

CHRIS: *(keeping her distance)*
Alright, I made a mistake, I admit. I never should've tried to blackmail you. I realize that now . . . Look, Steve, just let me go, and . . . Steve, you can't do this! Stop it!

STEVE:

Sorry, love. You see, you're the one person who could destroy everything. You're supposed to be dead. What if Pam spots you in some film? The way Tony remembered you from *Hangman's Noose*? What then? . . .

TONY has manoeuvred CHRIS close to the desk. Suddenly she remembers the gun. Desperate, she grabs it from the drawer and trains it on TONY.

CHRIS:

Stop right there, Tony. I don't want to use this, believe me I don't. But I will if you make me . . . *(TONY halts)* Now get out of my way, and you won't get hurt.

STEVE:

You don't think I'd keep a loaded gun in the house, do you, Chris? What sort of idiot do you take me for?

CHRIS:

You're saying the gun's not loaded?

STEVE:

Look for yourself.

CHRIS:

I have a much better idea. *(She turns the gun on STEVE)* On the count of three, I'll pull the trigger. Shall we find out which one of us is bluffing? One . . . two . . .

STEVE:

Drop the knife, Tony! Drop it, I said!

TONY tosses the knife on the desk.

CHRIS:

That's better. Now get out of my way, Tony.

TONY:

And what if I don't? Will you pull the trigger? You know, Steve, I don't think she will. I don't think she's got what it takes to shoot someone down in cold blood . . . *(He lunges at her. A struggle ensues, and the gun discharges. TONY drops to one knee, incredulous, the look on his face one of surprise, if not shock. His hand touches his chest in an almost tentative gesture as though he can't quite believe the red stain on his shirt. Then he looks at his hand, at his bloodied palm, the realization sinking in that he's been set up)* Man, oh, man, Steve, you are really something . . . *(He pulls himself to his feet and reaches for the knife but his knees buckle and he falls to the floor, dead)*

STEVE approaches. He kneels beside the body. Feels for a pulse. Lifts an eyelid.

STEVE: *(getting to his feet)*
He's dead. I'm afraid you've killed him.

CHRIS: *(trembling)*
It was an accident. You saw what happened. He attacked me. The gun went off . . .

Using his handkerchief, STEVE takes the gun from CHRIS'S hand.

STEVE:
Don't worry, it wasn't your fault. Tony and I rehearsed his death for hours.   *(He nudges TONY's foot with his toe)*   Didn't we, sport?

CHRIS:
Rehearsed? What do you mean? . . .

STEVE:
It was all a performance. You were supposed to shoot him when he lunged at you. Otherwise, he'd twist the gun towards himself and pull the trigger. He thought there were blanks in it, you see.

CHRIS:
Blanks? . . .

STEVE: *(crossing to the desk)*
He didn't quite make it onto the rug, I notice. (*He locks the gun in the drawer and pockets the key*) He looked so surprised, didn't he? As though he couldn't quite believe it. Poor Tony. Such a trusting soul. So gullible.

CHRIS:
Then you had no intention of harming me? That was just part of the setup?

STEVE:
Of course. It was all meant to make you shoot our budding author there. Or make you believe you had. In exchange for my getting rid of the body, you'd agree to stop the blackmail.

CHRIS:
But you doublecrossed him. Why?

STEVE:
Why? Because having underestimated you once. I wasn't about to do it again. No, I was afraid you'd see through the scam. Not in the heat of the moment, maybe, but later on. Then again, Tony knew too much. In the future he might have blackmailed me, much the way you were doing. That always worried me. And then one day the solution presented itself. All I had to do was substitute real bullets for blanks, and the rest would follow according to plan. That's why I just locked the murder weapon in the desk. It has your fingerprints on it . . . (*Using the handkerchief, he picks up the switch-blade, closes it, and slips it into the pocket of TONY's pants*) Here. Take his feet. I want to put him in the cellar. Tonight I'll dispose of the body . . . Well? What are you waiting for? Take his feet . . .

CHRIS:
No, I can't. I don't want to . . .

STEVE:
Alright, I'll do it myself . . .   *(He lifts TONY under the arms and begins to drag his body toward the hall)*   If I were you, Chris, I'd just go home and forget all this. You were never here today, right? As for Tony, who knows what happened to him? He just disappeared. Harry will write him off, and his Parole Officer will assume he had all he could take of living at home with Mother . . . *(He exits into the hall)*

> *As soon as he's gone, CHRIS darts to the desk and tests the drawer into which STEVE has put the gun. As STEVE said, it's locked . . . She picks up the steel letter-opener and attempts to pry open the drawer. Her attempts are futile . . . Knowing STEVE could return any second, she tosses down the letter-opener and moves to the coffee table. She scoops up the money and stuffs it into her purse. She then crosses to the French doors, opens them, and runs out . . . A moment later, STEVE walks in. Right away he sees the French doors are wide open and that CHRIS is no longer in the room. Then he notices the money is gone.*

STEVE:
Oh, well, I suppose I can't complain. Fifteen grand's not much, considering she's out of my hair for good . . . *(He crosses to the buffet and pours himself a drink)*

> *Just then, the real GEMMA DODD enters through the French doors. In her late twenties, she wears a sundress and sunglasses. On her head is a straw sunhat . . . (Note: under no circumstances should this character ever be played by the character playing CHRIS. In fact, GEMMA should always be played by a sixth cast member)*

GEMMA:
I see you bought a word processor. Does it make the
writing any easier?

STEVE:
Not really . . . You startled me. I didn't hear you come
in.

GEMMA: *(removing her sunglasses and hat)*
The doors were wide open . . . Oh, and in case you're
wondering, Chris doesn't know I'm here. To make a
long story short, I followed her. I've been twiddling my
thumbs in the gazebo. Just the way you taught me to in
the good old days.

STEVE:
What is it you want, Gemma?

GEMMA:
He's wondering to himself, 'How much does Gemma
know? How did she find out?'

STEVE:
How did you?

GEMMA:
Gustav Mahler. You see, this morning I was going to
listen to The Fourth Symphony —   *(She takes the
cassette from the pocket of her dress and tosses it on the desk)*
— and found something else entirely. The fact my
sister's become a blackmailer rather distresses me . . .
(She crosses to the buffet and pours herself a drink)   She
did a beautiful job on you, didn't she? All that rubbish
about cutting my wrists. That must've played on your
guilt, didn't it?

STEVE:

> She made that up?

GEMMA:

> I'm disappointed in you, Steve. I thought you were
> more astute than that.   *(She holds up her wrists)*
> There. No scars. Satisfied? . . . Do you really think my
> self-esteem depends on you or anyone else? . . .
> *(She carries her drink to the sofa and makes herself comfortable)*
> By the way, I read *Natural Causes* last week. Want to
> know what I thought?

STEVE:

> Not in particular.

GEMMA:

> You'll know soon enough. I'm reviewing it next week for
> the *Globe*. . . Basically, I say it's written the way some
> middle-aged men make love. It starts out well, loses
> focus in the middle, then picks up near the end.

STEVE:

> Don't you ever tire of putting down popular writers?
> What is it, Gemma? The curdled milk of envy? The fact
> you can't do it yourself?

GEMMA:

> I wouldn't even attempt it. I don't believe in demeaning
> myself.

STEVE:

> Right. I forgot. You'd rather turn out books that rarely
> make your publisher a dime. Well, in case you haven't
> noticed, lady, it's people like me who keep the publisher
> solvent in order to allow people like you the luxury of
> being a snob.

GEMMA:

That makes me a snob? Because I refuse to lower my standards?

STEVE:

Oh, come on. You think the reading public is a shallow lot, even vulgar. Only attracted by what is meretricious in a book. The literary equivalent of sex and car chases. A writer who believes that is in danger of disappearing in ever-diminishing circles up her own attitude. Oh, and before I forget, does the *Globe* know we used to be lovers? That fact alone might colour your review, don't you think?

GEMMA:

Perhaps you should write a letter to the editor. Denounce me for conflict of interest. And make sure you include all the sordid details of our affair. That should interest your wife.

STEVE:

You're behind the times, Gemma. Pam already knows about our sordid affair, as you so quaintly put it. I told her last week.

GEMMA:

I don't believe you.

STEVE:

That's your problem. When Chris threatened me with blackmail, I did the only smart thing I could do. I went straight to my wife and confessed. She wanted to call the Police, but I talked her out of it.

GEMMA:

Pam simply forgave you? Shrugged it off like a dent in her fender? Come on, Steve. You were always terrified she'd find out.

STEVE:

Believe what you want. Pam has her own agenda. It doesn't include conforming to stereotype.

GEMMA:

Then what was Chris doing here just now? That wasn't a friendly visit. I saw the way she ran out of here.

STEVE:

Chris dropped by to get her blackmail money. I laughed in her face. I told her Pam already knew, and if she didn't believe me, to just send her the tape. I also said if she wasn't out of my house by the time I picked up the phone, I'd call the Police . . .   *(He crosses to the desk and sits in front of his computer)*   So now if you'll excuse me, I'd like to get back to work.

Slight pause.

GEMMA:

Aren't you going to ask me what I've been working on?

STEVE:

I don't think so.

GEMMA:

It's not like my usual stuff at all. It's about obsession. A woman falls under a man's spell. They plot to murder his wife. The woman has an attack of conscience. The man drops her . . .

STEVE:

What do you want from me? Why did you come here?

GEMMA:

Maybe I just wanted to see you. Is that such a crime?

STEVE:

We had an affair, Gemma. An affair by definition is short.

GEMMA:

It's funny, isn't it? I never wanted to go to that wrap party. But Chris insisted. I remember asking one of the grips who that was leaning against the bar.'He's no actor,' he said. 'He's just the writer. If you want a leg up in this racket, love, chat up the producer.'

STEVE:

Grips are full of good advice.

GEMMA:

I felt I'd known you all my life. From the moment we met it was as if some bond existed between us. Some connection I didn't understand, but knew I would in future . . .

STEVE:

Nonsense. That's all in your mind.

GEMMA:

Romantic rubbish. I agree . . . And yet why do I still feel it, Steve? Still see the quarry in my dreams? Sometimes it frightens me.

STEVE:

It didn't frighten you the night we first made love.

GEMMA:

That was different. I felt so alive that night. So totally alive. We had the top down. The wind was in our hair, and the moon followed behind us like a lamp. Remember? . . . All the way up there I kept thinking, this is the man I've been waiting for. My soul mate. I'm sitting here beside him now. And I don't give a fig if he's married or not. Please, God, I just want to be with him. Even if it's just for one night.

STEVE:

One night is never enough, is it?

GEMMA:

The quarry spooked me at first. In the moonlight the white rocks looked like tombstones, and the water was black and deep . . . I remember every detail.

STEVE:

Cut the purple prose, Gemma. You know perfectly well why the quarry frightens you. It's where we planned on hiding Pam's body. Even in daylight the place feels haunted.

GEMMA:

No, it's more than that, Steve. It's as if our destinies — yours and mine — are somehow still linked to that place. That's why I keep having those dreams. I know it . . .

Just then, TONY bounds into the room. He has washed the fake blood off his hands and is buttoning up a clean shirt.

TONY:

Man, oh, man, Steve, I gotta hand it to you, it worked. How 'bout that? . . .   *(Suddenly he notices GEMMA)* Oh. Oh, sorry, Steve. I didn't realize you had company . . .

STEVE:

I thought I told you to stay upstairs? What's wrong with you? Don't you ever listen?

TONY:

It's just that I saw Chris go down the drive. I didn't hear anyone else come in . . .   *(To GEMMA)*   Hey, don't I know you? Sure. You're Susan Wakefield, aren't you? I saw you signing books last year. At Britnell's, wasn't it?

GEMMA:

My God, what a memory!

STEVE:

That's nothing. He remembers kids he went to kindergarten with. Don't you, sport?

TONY:

It's just something I was born with, Ms. Wakefield. Part of my DNA. I think I got it from my father, he was a cop. By the way, I'm Anthony. Anthony Bishop.   *(He shakes hands)*   I'm real pleased to meet you.

STEVE:

Tony, Susan Wakefield's a pen name. Her real name's Dodd. Gemma Dodd.

TONY:

Chris's sister? . . .

STEVE:

Precisely. Now run along.

TONY:

I'll just be outside, Steve. Dammit! Why can't I keep my mouth shut?   *(He exits into the garden)*

GEMMA:

What a strange man. Who is he?

STEVE: *(crossing to the desk)*
My protégé and garage mechanic. Wants to write thrillers in the worst way. He'd poison his poor Mom to win a Silver Dagger, let alone a Gold. *(He unlocks the drawer)*

GEMMA:
Really? . . . *(Curious, she wanders over to the mantle, takes down the Silver Dagger, and examines it)* It is lovely, isn't it? Rather elegant.

STEVE:
Mmm . . . *(Next, he opens the drawer, quietly empties the blanks from the gun, and inserts real bullets, all done unobtrusively as GEMMA is otherwise absorbed)*

GEMMA:
Just for the record, Steve, it was pills I took that night. I don't know why Chris said I'd cut my wrists. Wasn't dramatic enough for her, I suppose . . . *(She puts back the Silver Dagger and picks up a picture of PAM, studying it)* God, I was such a mess. I thought of calling the Police. I even considered calling your wife. 'Pam, honey, I'd change your will if I were you. That husband of yours wants you dead.'

STEVE:
Actually, I'm glad you abandoned ship. Now I've come up with a better scheme. One in which I get what I want and Pam lives to a ripe old age. Want to hear it?

GEMMA:
I don't think so. The less I know about your plans, the better I like it. *(She returns the picture to the mantle and turns to face STEVE)*

STEVE:

It doesn't matter now . . . I just wish you hadn't come here today, Gemma. Now you've forced me into a corner. And there's only one way out. For me, anyway. *(He raises the gun and fires. GEMMA drops to the floor. TONY rushes in from the garden)*

TONY:

What happened, Steve? I thought I heard a . . .   *(He notices the gun in STEVE's hand, then spots the body on the floor. TONY bends down and checks for vital signs)*   She's dead . . .

STEVE:

I had to do it, Tony. She might've told her sister she saw you here. You can see the consequences of that, can't you? All Chris had to do to get her revenge was contact Pam. Then it would've been game over.

TONY:

I know, but . . . Jesus, Steve, don't you realize what you've done? This isn't make-believe anymore. You've actually killed her. I can't believe it. You've actually killed the woman.

Blackout.

SCENE TWO

Ten days later. Night.

The drapes are open, and moonlight streams into the room.

At the desk, STEVE sits in front of his word processor, tapping happily on the keys.

The phone rings. STEVE continues to write. The phone rings once more before the answering machine clicks on. Then we hear —

CHRIS' VOICE:
Steve, this is Chris. I know you're there. Pick up the phone . . . Alright, if that's the way you want it, I'm coming over . . .

STEVE stops writing, pushes back from the computer, and reaches for the phone. But CHRIS has hung up. STEVE dials her number, listens, then slams down the handset.

STEVE:
Dammit.

Doorbell.

STEVE:
Christ, what is this? The Stock Exchange?   *(He exits into the hall, only to return a few seconds later with TONY. He is dressed in his leather jacket and blue jeans)*   Look, whatever it is, Tony, let's make it brief. Chris's on her way over. Needless to say I don't want her bumping into you.

TONY:
What does she want?

STEVE:
She didn't say. I assume it's not to return the fifteen grand she stole.

TONY:
You alone, Steve?

STEVE:
What does it look like? Of course I'm alone. Pam's not due back till the week-end . . . *(He takes in TONY, as though for the first time)* My God, what's wrong? You look terrible.

TONY:
I'll tell you what's wrong. I haven't had a decent night's sleep in ages. Not since . . . *(He practically shivers)*

STEVE:
I thought we agreed not to mention Gemma? *(He crosses to the buffet and pours a rye)*

TONY:
I can't help it. I dreamt I was picking up Police calls on the bedpost. Do you suppose that's what they mean by a guilty conscience?

STEVE:
I think it's what they mean by a vivid imagination.

TONY:
It nearly cost me my job. I forgot to tighten the lug nuts on a back wheel, and it almost fell off. The guy was doing sixty past the cemetery. Lucky for him he heard the lug nuts knocking around inside the hubcap . . .

STEVE: *(hands TONY the rye)*
Here. Drink this.

TONY:

> The worst thing is I haven't been able to write. Not a goddamn word, Steve. Not a comma.

STEVE:

> Look, most writers experience dry spells. It happens to me with every book.

TONY:

> Dry spells? Steve, I'm only on chapter three. Choking this early in the game is like standing at the plate with a full count. The pitcher's winding up and you just know he's going to throw a slider or a fork ball . . .   (*He belts back the rye*)

STEVE:

> Stop thinking baseball, dammit.

TONY:

> Twice now I've seen her in my dreams. Once she was standing beside the bed. I noticed a large red rose embroidered on her blouse. Only it wasn't a rose, and it wasn't embroidery, it was . . .   (*This time he shivers*)

STEVE:

> Stop it, Tony. You've got to get hold of yourself. This is all in your mind . . . For God's sake, you didn't kill Gemma, I did. You didn't even help get rid of the body. You don't even know where she's buried.

TONY:

> Maybe not. But I have a pretty good idea.

STEVE:

> Besides, no one knows what happened here that day. No one but the two of us.

TONY:
Jesus, why did you kill her, Steve? Why?

STEVE:
You know why.

TONY:
That's just it, I don't. Not really. I mean, your books are beginning to make you a name. You don't need all this . . .   *(He gestures to include the room)*

STEVE:
I suppose I could live modestly on my royalties. The trouble is I've grown accustomed to luxury. Wouldn't you rather be able to write exactly what you want for the rest of your life and not have to worry about making a living? That, dear Tony, is what Gemma threatened to deprive me of. Does that answer your question?

TONY:
It does. Let's just see if I got it all . . .   *(He removes a pocket-sized tape recorder from inside his jacket. He presses the rewind button, then the play button)*

STEVE'S VOICE:
. . . For God's sake, you didn't kill Gemma, I did. You didn't even help get rid of the body. You don't even know where she's buried —

> *TONY stops the tape. Tucks the tape recorder back into his jacket.*

TONY:
Aren't the Japanese ingenious?

STEVE: *(approaches TONY)*
Hand it over.

TONY: *(producing the switchblade)*
Sorry, Steve. All rights are reserved, including the right to reproduce this tape, or portions thereof, in any form. So help me God.

STEVE:
I thought we were friends?

TONY:
We are. That doesn't mean I'm brain-dead. You see, Steve, I've decided that what you don't know about intrigue could fit on the head of a pin, along with all those angels.

STEVE:
What? You think I'd betray you?

TONY:
In a second. That's why I sold you a bill of goods. You really ate it up, didn't you? All that crap about lug nuts and nightmares. The truth is my book's almost writing itself. A real page-turner, *par excellence.*

STEVE:
Oh, you'll do well on the book circuit, Tony. Don't forget *de rigeur* and *au courant.*

TONY:
The tape goes into a safe-deposit box. It's my insurance policy. Just in case you hatch some plan to pin Gemma's murder on me. Understand? . . .

Doorbell.

STEVE:
That's Chris . . .   *(Indicates the French doors)*   Go
out this way . . .

TONY: *(halts in the open doorway)*
One thing, Steve. You know the title of your work-in-progress? I've been meaning to tell you: it stinks.

STEVE:
Oh? What's wrong with it?

TONY:

Shouldn't a title be more evocative? Even metaphorical? *Murder On The Village Green* sounds like the Golden Age of English cozies. Remember those? The vicar is found face down in the library, dead from a rare poison found only in a fish under the Polar Ice Cap. Enter Hornswoggle of the Yard . . .   *(He exits)*

STEVE: *(yells out the French doors)*
Besides, it's only a working title, you ungrateful little shit . . .   *(Again the doorbell chimes)*   Alright, I'm coming. Keep your shirt on . . . *(He exits into the hall, leaving one of the French doors open. Then we hear STEVE say)*   Pam. My God. You're back.

PAM: *(off)*
Hello, Steven. I forgot my key. Help the man with the bags, would you?

> *PAM sweeps into the library, glowing with good health. She's wearing a lovely summer outfit, a wide-brimmed straw hat in her hand. She tosses the hat on the wing chair and picks up her mail, glancing through it. The front door bangs shut and STEVE appears in the hallway. He sets down the luggage and enters the library, still in shock. He watches PAM.*

PAM:

> The ride from the airport almost undid ten days in St. Marten. Not quite, thank God. Not even the crazies on the road could manage that . . . Well, don't just stand there. Say something. Do I look different?

STEVE:

> You're four days early, aren't you? . . .

PAM:

> There's a reason for that. But first, I want to tell you what happened at the conference. I had the greatest piece of luck. Just before the keynote address, Professor Levin of Princeton was rushed to the hospital. Apparently he ate some tainted shellfish.

STEVE:

> Professor Levin? Wasn't he the designated speaker?

PAM:

> Exactly. Now do you get the picture?

STEVE:

> Let me guess. The moment you heard about Levin's misfortune, you dashed to the organizing committee and volunteered to fill in.

PAM:

> Am I that transparent?

STEVE:

> When the program change was announced, the audience was delirious. All one hundred academics stood up and cheered.

PAM:

Can you blame them? His topic was: 'Death and Adultery in the Post-War Novel.' Mine, as you know, was: 'Sex and Violence in Detective Fiction.' Which would you rather sit through? . . .   *(Suddenly CHRIS steps into the open doorway. STEVE notices her just before she turns and disappears)*   What's the matter? You look as though I'd caught you with another woman . . .

STEVE:

You're not far wrong. I was hard at work on my new novel, *Body Count*. You know how demanding my muse can be. Unless I give her my full attention, she tends to go elsewhere.

PAM:

In that case, I won't distract you. Besides, I want to take a hot bath, then unpack . . .   *(She starts to go, then stops)*   Oh, I might as well tell you now why I'm home early. I met someone in St. Marten. I plan on seeing him again.

STEVE:

A lover? I don't believe it.

PAM:

I had every intention of staying the full week, but Arthur had to return to Princeton on business.

STEVE:

Arthur? Good God. Don't tell me you gave Professor Levin a tumble? I thought he'd taken to his deathbed?

PAM:

He had. But I took some roses to his room and he sprang to life. Even the nurses were amazed at the quick recovery . . .   *(She exits upstairs)*

STEVE:
I always wondered what academics did with all that free time. Now I know . . . *(STEVE crosses to the French doors. He is met by CHRIS)* Damn you, Chris. Don't you realize the danger you've put me in? Lucky for me you didn't ring the bloody doorbell.

CHRIS:
Luck's got nothing to do with it. I saw the limo pull into the driveway.

STEVE:
Alright, but you have to go. I can't talk here. Not now. It's far too risky.

CHRIS:
I'm not going anywhere, Steve. I want to know what's happened to Gemma, and I'm not leaving here till I find out.

STEVE:
I don't know what you're talking about. Gemma? Has something happened to her?

CHRIS:
Don't screw me around, alright? I drove up to Lake Simcoe today. No one up there has seen her for at least a week. Ten days, to be exact.

STEVE:
So?

CHRIS:
So she was supposed to be hard at work, correcting her manuscript. In fact, the book is still at the cabin . . . The kid at the Esso station remembers the last time he saw her. She was on her way to town . . . and dropped by to get gas. He remembers because it was his birthday . . .

Guess what day that was, Steve? The day Pam flew off to
St. Marten. The day I was here last. Remember that?

STEVE:

And no one has seen her since?

CHRIS:

That's right. Her publisher called this morning.
Gemma was supposed to deliver her novel at ten. That's
why I drove up to the cabin . . . You know what else I
discovered up there Steve? Besides the partially
corrected manuscript?

STEVE:

What?

CHRIS:

Her Sony Walkman.

STEVE:

I don't understand.

CHRIS:

The Walkman wasn't supposed to be at the cabin. She'd
forgotten it when she left town. She'd also forgotten her
tapes. Which is why I was able to use Mahler the day I
blackmailed you.

STEVE:

I see. In other words, how did her Walkman get to the
cabin?

CHRIS:

Very good, Inspector. Now should I tell you what I think
happened? The only sequence of events that makes any
sense?

STEVE:
> By all means.

CHRIS:
> Let's begin with the night we pulled that sting on Pam.
> When I got home from here, I tossed the tape on the
> shelf and forgot about it. Mainly because Gemma was
> out of town . . . Then sometime in the following week,
> she must've driven in for some reason — maybe a
> dentist's appointment — and dropped by the house.
> She picked up the Walkman and some tapes, including
> Mahler, and drove back to the country.

STEVE:
> Sheer speculation.

CHRIS:
> Let me finish . . . Then one morning she leaps out of
> bed and decides it's time to jog. She slips on her track
> suit, puts The Fourth Symphony in the Walkman, and
> starts off through the woods. Only it's not Mahler she
> hears, suddenly, but the musical strains of extortion.
> Her little sister blackmailing her ex-lover.

STEVE:
> So you think she drove in again to confront one of us? . . .
> Next you'll be saying she followed you here and hid in
> the gazebo till you left.

CHRIS:
> Alright, so I'm speculating. All I know is Gemma would
> want to get to the bottom of it. She must've brought the
> tape with her. It's not at the cabin and it's not at our
> house . . . I can see how furious the tape would've made
> her. Not only was I blackmailing you, I was guilty of
> plagiarism, so to speak.

STEVE:
Plagiarism? What do you mean?

CHRIS:
Just that. I stole the idea of blackmail from Gemma's new book. She'd finally taken your advice, Steve, and tried her hand at something different. It's a thriller, called *Silver Dagger.*

STEVE:
A thriller?

CHRIS:
And wait till you hear this . . . The characters are a slightly sinister mystery writer, his lover, a novelist of great integrity, and the novelist's young sister, a film actress. At one point, the actress blackmails our hero.

PAM: *(off)*
Steven.

STEVE: *(to CHRIS, sotto voce)*
Quick. The curtain.

> *CHRIS positions herself behind the drapes as PAM comes down the stairs and into the room. She wears a dressing gown.*

PAM: *(glances around)*
That's funny. I thought I . . . Were you just talking to someone?

> *Just then, STEVE notices CHRIS' purse on the floor beside the end of the sofa. He deftly moves to nudge it out of PAM's sightline with his foot.*

STEVE:
Oh, that. No, I was rattling on to myself. Trying out some dialogue.

PAM:
Oh. I could've sworn . . . Never mind. Bring my suitcases upstairs, would you? They're too heavy for me to carry . . .   *(Then)*   You're sure you're alright?

STEVE:
Yes, of course. It's just the work. You know.

> *PAM nods. She glances around once more, then turns and goes upstairs.*

CHRIS: *(comes out from behind the drapes)*
That was too close for comfort.

STEVE: *(thrusts the purse at her)*
Just go. That's the second time tonight you almost got caught . . . And listen, I haven't the faintest idea where your sister is. I had no contact with her ten days ago, and I haven't seen her since. Nor do I expect to see her in future. Is that clear? . . .   *(CHRIS exits. STEVE closes the French doors, then exits into the hall. He picks up the suitcases and carries them upstairs)*

> *CHRIS enters through a different set of French doors and crosses to the desk. From her purse she takes out a set of skeleton keys and begins to try each one in the locked drawer, one eye on the stairway. Just as she spots STEVE returning, she tries another key and it works. She opens the drawer and grabs the gun, just as STEVE enters the room.*

CHRIS:
Hold it right there, Steve . . .   *(With the gun on STEVE, she searches the drawer, finds the tape)*   Now what have we here? Why, it's Mahler's Fourth. I wonder

how that got in your desk? . . . And what are these? . . .
(She holds up a pair of sunglasses)   Gemma's
sunglasses.

STEVE:
Those are Pam's, not Gemma's.

CHRIS:
Sorry, Steve. I was with Gemma the day she bought
them.

STEVE: *(moves about, but keeps his distance)*
You shouldn't have come here tonight, Chris. That
really was a mistake, you know. But you're just like your
sister, aren't you? Always getting in over your head.

CHRIS:
Where is she, Steve? What have you done with her?

STEVE:
Alright. Yes, Gemma was here that day. Right after you
left. She'd discovered the tape and wanted to talk about
it. The trouble is we didn't get that far because just
about then good old Tony bounded into the room. Or
blundered might be a better word.

CHRIS:
Tony? . . . You mean, he's not dead? I didn't kill him?

STEVE:
I'm beginning to wish you had. Now he expects me to
recommend his book to my publisher, plus write a
blurb for the dustjacket. No, I'm afraid Tony's death
was carefully scripted. Blanks and all. The same blanks
that're in the gun you're holding now . . .   *(CHRIS
drops the gun on the desk and snatches up the steel letter-
opener)*   A much simpler sting than the night I had

you play Gemma. Simpler, but just as effective . . .
(STEVE keeps moving, circling her)

CHRIS:
You missed your calling, Steve. Maybe you should
direct plays.

STEVE:
Very funny . . . Don't you want to know why I'm indulging
you like this? It must have occurred to you how
dangerous you've suddenly become. What if you went to
the Police? That tape might help convict me of murder.
Providing Gemma's body were ever found . . . *(He
scoops up the gun from the desk and trains it on CHRIS)*
By the way, I lied. The gun had blanks in it when Tony
and I staged his death, but later on I replaced them
with real bullets. You see, I couldn't let Gemma live. Not
when she might reveal that Tony was still alive. That
would've brought down the whole house of cards,
wouldn't it? . . . None of that matters now, of course.
Finding that tape was your second mistake of the night,
and your last . . .

CHRIS: *(backing away)*
You wouldn't do anything here, Steve. Not with your
wife in the house. You wouldn't dare.

STEVE:
I wouldn't worry about my wife if I were you. Right now
she's up to her jet lag in bubble bath. Probably half
asleep in the tub . . . *(He picks up a throw cushion
from the sofa and holds it against the gun to silence the shot)*
Anyway, she's not likely to hear a thing, is she?

PAM: *(appears in the doorway)*
Wrong, Steven. It seems your wife is not the fool you
think she is. She's been standing in the hall and heard
everything. Oh, I've got to hand it to you. That's quite a

rep company you have. You really had me convinced I'd seen a murder. Remind me to congratulate Tony. I take it he was part of the cast . . . As for you, Christine, I think you definitely have a future. Perhaps you can stage *The Mousetrap* in a penal institution. With an all-female cast, of course.

STEVE:

Please. Spare us the sarcasm.

PAM:

You know what angers me the most, Steven? The fact I was so naive, so gullible. I should've suspected something, shouldn't I? The moment you suggested we rescind the Marriage Contract?

STEVE:

Don't be too hard on yourself. I thought I handled the whole thing quite subtly . . .   *(Indicates CHRIS)* However, we do have a problem here. We can't just allow Chris to walk away, can we? She simply knows too much.

PAM:

What do you mean? You're not going to hurt her now, are you? I won't allow it, Steven. Put down the gun.

CHRIS:

If it's the tape you want, Steve, take it. Here. I don't want it. And I won't say anything. I won't go to the Police. I give you my word.

STEVE:

We can't risk it, Pam. She can't be trusted, and you know it. We both have too much at stake to let her ruin us . . .   *(He aims the gun at CHRIS)*

CHRIS:
 You bastard! What about Gemma? What did you do with her body?

STEVE:
 Alright. There's an old abandoned quarry not far from our cottage. Pam knows it. Gemma's in the trunk of her car. In twenty feet of water.

PAM:
 My God.

STEVE:
 Strange, isn't it? I took her there once, and it spooked her. It was almost as though she sensed her own death . . .
 (He fires. CHRIS barely flinches. He fires again)

CHRIS:
 Don't waste your time, shithead. They're all blanks.
 (She pulls a pistol from her purse and trains it on STEVE)
 This one, however, fires real bullets. Sit down.

PAM:
 Don't look so surprised, Steven. Did you think you were the only one who could pull off something like this? You forget I'm your wife. I know how that mind of yours works.

STEVE:
 You and Chris planned all this together? That's impossible. How? When?

PAM:
 Actually, I've been back for some time. I've been staying at Jane's. Oh, and in case you're wondering, Professor Levin did get sick and I did fill in. All that's true. Alas, we were never lovers. That I made up.

STEVE:
How disappointing for you.

PAM:
On the contrary. I was worried you might have phoned the hotel and found I'd checked out. The Professor was my cover story.

CHRIS:
Did you like the skeleton keys? Don't you think I carried that off well? Pretending to be caught in the act?

STEVE:
Obviously you'd already replaced the bullets with blanks. Which means you already knew the tape and glasses were in the drawer . . . You mind if I get a drink?

PAM:
Help yourself . . .   *(As STEVE crosses to the buffet and*
pours himself a Scotch)   You must be wondering how I
found you out.

STEVE:
How did you?

PAM:
It was Jane who stumbled onto it, actually. The day after I arrived at St. Marten, she called the hotel. She still hadn't destroyed the Pre-nuptial, she said, and had no intention of doing so. Not till she'd done some snooping on her own.

STEVE:
Let me guess. She wanted the name of the woman I'd supposedly murdered. To check her out.

PAM:

Exactly. The next day she called again. It seemed there was no Gemma Dodd working for Air Canada. Never had been. In fact, the only Gemma Dodd in the phone book was a writer.

STEVE:

How did she know that?

PAM:

Simple. She called the number.

CHRIS:

It was early in the morning. I was half asleep. She asked if I was Gemma. I said, 'No, this is Chris.' I told her Gemma was at the cabin, working on her book. 'Sorry,' she said, 'Wrong Gemma Dodd. I'm looking for a flight attendant.' That's when I came fully awake.

PAM:

Jane simply reported the conversation to me. She had no idea that Chris was supposed to be dead. The fact she was still alive only proved I'd been the victim of a cruel hoax . . . Two days later I flew back and knocked on Chris's door. As it happens, she was just about to drive up to the cabin and look for her sister. I went along.

CHRIS:

We found the manuscript and the Walkman, but no Mahler and no Gemma. We figured she'd listened to the tape and gone to see you, taking the tape with her.

PAM:

So one day while you were out, we let ourselves in and began to search the house. The first place I looked was your desk. Lo and behold, the tape was in the locked drawer, along with the sunglasses.

STEVE:

I should've gotten rid of all that. How careless of me . . . It was probably the sunglasses, wasn't it, even more than the tape, that made you suspect foul play?

PAM:

That's right. That's why we drove to the cottage and dug up the garden. If you had done away with Gemma, that seemed as good a place as any to bury the body.

STEVE:

I'm not that stupid, Pam. That's the first place you or Chris would think to look.

PAM:

No, you're right. That's when I knew I'd have to beat you at your own game. If I could prove you'd really murdered Gemma, I'd be out from under your thumb once and for all . . . What I needed was a plan. And just as I was thinking this, something happened that made it all possible . . . *(She casually pushes open the French doors as if to let in the night)* Chris and I were having lunch at a sidewalk café, when her face went white and she knocked over her glass. 'It's him!' she said. 'Look!'

STEVE:

Who?

PAM:

Why, Tony, of course. There he was, strolling along the sidewalk. I didn't know what all the fuss was about. But then I didn't know he'd been shot dead the afternoon I left for the Caribbean. Another of your master strokes . . .

TONY enters through the French doors.

TONY:

Sorry, Steve. Your wife threatened to tell my Parole Officer what I'd been up to. That's why I had to go along with them, I swear.

STEVE:

I have to hand it to you, Tony. You were quite convincing. I bought it all, even the arrogance.

TONY:

Thanks, Steve. I guess I had a good teacher.

PAM:

Tony's role was the simplest part of the sting. To tape a murder confession from you. To make it look as though he'd gotten it to protect himself. Our job, Chris and mine, was to find where Gemma was buried. It took us a while before we hit upon the answer. What we had to do was create the right context for a confession — such as a second murder.

CHRIS:

Mine, as it turned out.

PAM:

I knew you'd be out yesterday. According to your date-book, you were getting your picture taken for that piece in *Saturday Night.* So while you were standing around the cemetery, dry ice up to your knees, we were here rehearsing. Much the way you'd done before with Chris and Tony . . . Well, I believe that just about covers it, don't you? I don't think I've left any loose ends.

STEVE:

Just one. What do you plan to do now, exactly? You know you can't turn me in. That's too costly an option.

PAM:

Have I mentioned the Police? No, I'll tell you what I'm going to do, Steven, and I don't want any argument. For starters, I want you out of this house tonight. Understand?

STEVE:

Tonight?

PAM:

That's right, tonight. You can stay at the cottage until the fall. No one will think it odd, your moving to the country. Writers need solitude to work . . . As soon as I get my promotion, we'll announce the divorce. There'll be no financial settlement, of course. Not a red cent. Just count yourself lucky you're not finishing your new novel behind bars . . . And if you try anything funny in the future, that's exactly where you'll end up. As for Chris and Tony, I'll make it worth their while to remain silent. Chris, for one, is a pragmatist, aren't you, Chris? She's already agreed not to say anything.

CHRIS:

I don't see what good I can do Gemma now. So why blow the whistle? . . .

The phone rings. STEVE goes to answer it, but PAM stops him. While he is at the desk, he furtively slips the steel letter-opener up his sleeve.

PAM: *(into the phone)*
Hello . . . Oh, hi, Jane . . . What? . . . Are you sure? . . . When? . . . They actually said that? . . . And there's no

mistake? They're positive? . . . Yes, alright . . . Yes, thanks, Jane . . .   *(She hangs up)*   Dammit.

CHRIS:
What is it? What's the matter?

PAM:
Jane just saw it on the news. They've found it, Steven. They just raised Gemma's car from the quarry.

STEVE:
That's impossible. They can't have found it. It's in twenty feet of water. No one ever goes there.

PAM:
Well, someone went there today. Two teenage boys. They were out hiking and went for a swim . . . The police have found a body in the trunk.

CHRIS:
Silver Dagger will be your undoing, Steve. The book has scenes that will lead the police straight to this house.

STEVE:
She said our destinies — hers and mine — were somehow linked to that place. My God, not only did she sense her own death, but she knew I'd be punished for it . . .
(In one swift movement, he slips behind TONY, seizes him around the neck, and brings the letter-opener close to his face)
Give me the recorder, Tony. Now.

TONY:
Hey, Steve, come on —

STEVE:
Now, I said! Hand it over!

TONY slips him the recorder. All the time, CHRIS has the gun trained on STEVE as he leads TONY slowly toward the French doors.

PAM:

You won't get away with it, Steven. You know that, don't you? Too much has happened.

STEVE:

We'll see about that. Without this confession, what do you have? Just my word against Tony's. And who will the Police sooner believe? An ex-con or an award-winning author? So you can kiss that promotion goodbye, Pam. Especially when I'll testify it was you who shot Gemma. *(He shoves TONY to the floor and darts out into the garden, disappearing into the night.)*

TONY: *(picking himself up)*
Good old Steve. He never gives up, does he? Always outsmarting his opponents. Drink anyone? . . .
(PAM shakes her head, worried. CHRIS puts away the gun and sits. TONY picks up his glass.)   Listen, don't look like that. He's not going to get away with it. It's just not in the cards. Steve was right about Gemma. She predicted he'd pay for his crime, and he will.

CHRIS:

What makes you say that?

PAM:

Yes, Tony. How can you be so cocksure?

TONY:

How? Simple . . . You see, Steve may have my Sony tape recorder, Mrs. Marsh, but *I* still have the tape.   *(He produces the tape cassette from his pants pocket and holds it up triumphantly)*   *That*'s how.

Blackout.